# CALLING MR. BEIGE

## Book One of the Shuttlecocks Series

Brian Harris

# CHAPTER ONE

"Hi!" said a scratchy female voice, interrupting Tad from his *Discover* magazine. Looking up from his seat in the library, Tad found a smiling young woman standing about ten feet away and giving the impression of staring straight at him. She wore dental headgear and her red hair thrust out in two asymmetrical bobtails, making him think of Pippi Longstocking. Clashing with the bobtails, was her pink halter-top emblazoned with the name ANGELA in white block letters. She was carrying a boombox, unusual, especially considering the surroundings.

Tad returned to his magazine article. It was about something called string theory and how the theory predicts the existence of multiple dimensions beyond length, width, height and time. Although one can't directly comprehend these added dimensions, they might have a profound impact on our universe. One of the scientists, from Berkeley, speculated that they might harbor the human soul.

Tad looked up again. The woman had still not moved and continued to stare in his direction. Her metallic smile widened. Tad turned around, scanning the West LA library, but nobody was behind him. His breath quickened. Could she have been talking to him? But why? He hadn't yelled at her. He hadn't shaken her. He was just reading a magazine.

"I said hi," said the woman.

#

"There he is!" A cry went up among the crowd assembled outside the West Hollywood movie theater. Emerging from the theater were actor Tad Mortriciano, his lawyer girlfriend of five years Laurie Hammer and manager Holden Ferere. They had just finished viewing a sneak preview of Tad's latest movie *Culture Vulture*. "Tad, we love you!"

"Hey!" Tad said, as a middle-aged woman with spiky yellow hair yanked off his $350 Gucci sunglasses, tearing through the crowd.

The three of them stumbled towards Holden's red Tesla, parked a half block away.

"I want to have your baby Tad!" remarked a heavy-set, severely pierced woman. A variety of items, including intimate apparel were thrust at Tad, with Holden snatching up a few. Holden and Laurie piled into the car, followed by Tad collapsing into the back seat beside Laurie.

"Hot! You're so hot Tad!" observed Holden.

"I don't like how they all ignore me," said Laurie, flinging her dirty blonde hair, her red roots showing. "I should have punched that fat one with the cornrows."

"I always mention you in the interviews," said Tad, absently rubbing the nail marks dug into his left arm.

"There is a way to make it clearer that I'm with you," she said, causing Tad's face to morph into that of a deer, in the headlights. "No pressures," she added hastily.

"Laurie, you know how I feel about you. Once things calm down—"

"No pressures! . . ."

"So I guess I'll drop you both off at Tad's?" asked Holden, adding, "Whenever you're ready."

"Huh?" asked Tad, breaking off the kiss. "Oh, yeah, but stop a block away. Marshmallow knows your car." Marshmallow was Tad's 120 pound Bouvier des Flandres

4

mix, rescued from the Santa Monica shelter six months before. Unfortunately, the dog did not come with any instructions or warnings, such as "ambush specialist."

After Holden dropped them off, Tad guided Laurie around the back door. Gently turning the key, he poked open the door. "Don't turn on the light," Tad whispered.

Laurie nodded, removing her shoes. The goal was to make it into the kitchen. There they could close the door and wait the dog out, perhaps share a cup of coffee until his energy level eased to a manageable level. Feeling around the couch, Tad turned the knob to the kitchen door. The door exploded from the inside, unleashing a dark blur accompanied by a grunt, and Tad was down as the dog licked his face.

"Tad," Laurie pointed at the digital clock on his answering machine, once the dog's greetings had subsided to a frenzied tail-wagging.

Tad glanced at the readout. 8:37. He was supposed to call his mother at 8:00. Every night. 8:00. Picking up the phone, he noticed the machine flashing 23 messages. Not too bad he thought, considering half were probably from his mother.

"I'm sorry—"

"Tad! Are you all right?"

"I'm fine."

"Let me get the police off the other line."

"The police! Mom? . . . She's called the police!" Laurie nodded, pointing again to the digital clock.

"Tad, thank god!" His mother was back on the line.

"The police?"

"I tried calling you. Where have you been?"

"I was at a screening Mom. There were a lot of previews. I lost track."

"Are you trying to kill me?"

"I'm absolutely not trying to kill you--"

"Because that's what you're doing you know."

"I'm sorry—"

"I thought you were kidnapped."

"Kidnapped!"

"You know all the crazies out there. That stalker, she almost killed Robert Downey Jr.."

"Nobody's stalking me."

"I guess that's too much to expect from you. One phone call."

"No, it's not too much to expect."

"You never visit. I'm a shut-in."

"You make yourself a shut-in. You've got a car."

"Tell me what happened today. I want to know everything."

Twenty-minutes later, he finally coaxed his mother off the phone. Making sure not to trip over Marshmallow, he walked into the bedroom, hoping Laurie was not yet asleep. Unfortunately, he was out of luck. That night Tad slept fitfully and awoke in a cold sweat. Laurie was looking down at him, her bleach blonde hair touching his face.

"Sweetheart," said Laurie. "You were shouting."

"A nightmare. I had a nightmare. I never have nightmares."

"Would you like to tell me about it?"

"It was awful. My eyeballs were on fire, there were tiny red crabs crawling all over my body, I was eating snakes—"

"It's over now," she said hastily. Rolling him over, she added "How about a backrub to ease your mind?"

She felt his breathing ease. "That's funny. I think it looks a little darker."

"What?" asked Tad, his body tensing.

"Your birthmark, the little shuttlecock," she replied. "Don't be so touchy. I think it's cute," she said.

#

Tad entered Tweezers at 3:15 and scanned the bar for Holden. The TV was set to CNN, which was reporting on a two-day long hostage situation in the Sherman Oaks Galleria. He spotted Holden at the opposite end of the bar.

"Sorry," Tad said, "I got held up at the doctor's."

Holden had an office, but Tad never recalled actually being in it. Holden preferred to hold his meetings in trendy hotspots, where he could dilute the business with hobnobbing.

"Something serious I hope?" said Holden, sliding over a flat Anchor Steam.

"Just the dermatologist, wanted to look at a mole. It's fine."

"A mole?" said Holden, his eyes scanning the bar.

"More like a birthmark, a little one on my shoulder."

"The shuttlecock?  I thought that was a tattoo."

"Did we come here to discuss skin blemishes or movie roles?"

"Right, well there's a little problem, *Blackbeard* is scheduled to begin shooting August 18th and *Stick in the Eye* August 20th."

"Yes?"

"So you can't do both."

"I don't recall signing contracts for either."

"You're their man. That's what both directors say. We're just waiting on the Netflix cuts."

"Well make it *Blackbeard* then. At least it's got some nuance to it. Speaking of which, did you see Morris' review in the Reporter?"

"I heard it was OK."

"Did you read what he wrote about me? Understated? An understated performance? I killed 34 people in that movie, 8 by chainsaw."

"True, but compared to *Hopalong Cannibal*—"

"I'm trying to put that one behind me."

"I'm putting it in the bank. $215 million box and *Vulture*'s going to do even better," observed Holden. "I think you've been spotted."

Holden nodded in the direction of two Texas-haired women who had just sat down on the opposite end of the bar. The women were smiling in their direction, whispering between themselves, smiling, and whispering, with a bit of hair twirling mixed in.

"Why do you insist on meetings in places like this?" asked Tad.

"Nothing wrong with mixing business with pleasure. This way I can get your leftovers."

"They're all leftovers. I'm serious about Laurie."

"Then why don't you tie the knot? Think of the free publicity."

"Holden, we haven't even been going out five years—"

The two women had paid for their drinks and were swaying over to their side of the bar.

"Hi, how are you two guys doing?" asked the taller, fluffier-haired one.

"Are you in the business?" asked the shorter, bustier one to Holden. "You look familiar."

"I'm an agent," stated Holden.

"That sounds so exciting," said the taller one.

"Bet you don't know who this is," Holden nodded in Tad's direction. Upon seeing their blank stares, Tad obligingly removed his new $15 drug store sunglasses.

"Are you an agent too?" asked the shorter one.

"This is Tad Mortriciano," said Holden, a bit perplexed.

"Tad Mort—oh, yeah!" said the short one.

"I've seen all your movies," said the tall one.

"We're here on business," Tad explained, retrieving his handy autograph pen. The women both thanked him for the pen, then promptly scribbled their phone numbers on a cocktail napkin, with the shorter one handing it to Holden. Smiling at Holden, they walked away.

#

8

Tad arrived home exhausted from the day-long film shoot in Calgary. There were only three shots where he was needed, but they took at least 10 takes each. The movie was a buddy werewolf story, but there didn't seem to be much chemistry between himself and Seth Rogen. The director was a known perfectionist and wasn't satisfied with the "impact" Tad was putting into his role. The filming, which was supposed to take two hours required the entire day and resulted in a missed flight and late arrival.

Unlocking the apartment, Tad turned on the light and tossed his day bag onto the couch. Marshmallow ambled up to greet him, his tail a slow metronome.

"Hiya Marshmallow, miss me?" Tad asked, scratching the dog behind his ears. Marshmallow replied with two cursory licks and his tail revved up a notch. The dog was eating well and showed no overt signs of sickness. Nevertheless, he appeared lethargic. Tad made a mental note to take him into the vet this week.

His message machine was flashing 12 messages, but that wasn't the number that worried him. What worried him was the clock which showed 8:57. The time change! Calgary was only one hour ahead, not two this time of year.

"Hello?" his mother answered. Good, at least she wasn't already at the police station.

"I'm sorry. I forgot."

"Oh yeah. I was wondering when you were going to call."

"My fault. The shoot ran long. The time change--"

"You're supposed to call at 8:00."

"I know, I'll be more careful."

"So tell me about your day."

When Tad woke up the next morning, he found himself scratching the birthmark on his shoulder, as if he were bitten by a mosquito. Inspecting it, he couldn't see anything amiss, although it perhaps looked a bit darker than before. He put on some of the lotion he got from the dermatologist which seemed to help. Padding into the living room, Tad played back his phone messages. Two were from Laurie, four were wrong numbers and six were from solicitors and electioneers. There was nothing from Holden though, who was supposed to call to finalize the *Blackbeard* contract. Tad wasn't too happy about this. Lately, Holden had appeared distracted, not nearly as solicitous as usual. Maybe he had some kind of personal problem that was bothering him. If so, he should have felt free to talk to Tad about it.

After two rings Holden's assistant answered, "Mr. Ferere's office. How can I help you?"

"Hi Fatima. It's Tad. Is Holden available?"

"Let me check."

"Hey buddy, what's going on."

"Hi Holden. Is your caller I.D. broken?"

"Broken? No, I don't think so."

"So why is Fatima picking up my call?"

"Oh. I was finalizing some contract details. The Catwoman sequel—*Return of the Whip!* I told Scarlett to go for the up-front and screw the residuals."

"Scarlett Johansson? Since when do you represent Scarlett Johansson?"

"Since last month, her contract with ICM was up. I thought I told you."

"No, I don't believe you did. That's very good."

An awkward pause followed. Surely he must know what I'm calling about, thought Tad.

"Holden, I didn't hear from you on the *Blackbeard* contract."

"Oh, yeah, they gave it to Depp."

"What? I thought it was in the bag."

"So did I, but what can you do? Depp's got this thing with pirates you know."

"Why didn't you call me?"

"I'm sorry. You're absolutely right. I was just so bogged down. I don't think that script was the right vehicle for you anyway."

"So I guess we'll go with *Stick in the Eye*?"

"Right! I'll get right on it Todd."

"Thanks—did you just call me Todd?"

"I meant Tad. Sorry, it's been a long day."

"It's 10:00 am." Tad noted before hanging up. Yes, there was something definitely up with Holden. He wondered if Holden was doing drugs.

Tad spent the rest of the morning loafing around the apartment and playing with Marshmallow. He tried to teach Marshmallow to shake hands, but the dog wasn't in the mood to obey any of his commands that day. He called Laurie at the office. She was swamped as usual with a case, but she was able to juggle some stuff so they could get together Thursday night. The afternoon he spent working out and jogging along Santa Monica park. Luckily, he was able to complete his workout and jog without being interrupted by the paparazzi. He did spot an old girlfriend at the gym, but she hadn't looked in his direction.

By the time he got back in the car it was 8:00 already. He had forgotten to call his mother again.

"It's me."

"I'm sorry?"

"Why are you sorry?"

"May I ask who's calling?"

"Mom, it's Tad. 8:00."

"Tad, I'm glad to hear from you. How are you doing?"

"Mom, are you feeling all right?"

"My elbow is acting up again. Why?"

"Nothing. You'll be happy to hear what happened today. Remember that *Blackbeard* project you were so upset about?"

"Yes, I don't like you in misogynist roles."

"Well I've got good news. It turns out they're going to go with Johnny—"

"That's nice. Look I'm right in the middle of vacuuming. Can you tell me about this tomorrow?"

#

"So you used to be an actor?" asked Dr. Fellows.

"Yes, but again I don't see how that matters."

"It matters because the feelings you're experiencing are common, actually quite typical for someone who's experienced a career change. It's not easy to give up being the center of attention. I have another patient, a newly retired CEO, with many of the same issues."

"My problem started before my career change."

"Let's try and focus on your problem. Tell me precisely what you've been feeling."

"It's a bit hard to explain. It's like I've become invisible."

"Well, I see you," Dr. Fellows glanced at his notes, "Tad, I see you very clearly."

"No, that's not it. Not invisible. It's more like nobody pays attention to me. They see me, but they just don't care."

"You sound alienated."

"You bet I'm alienated! Wouldn't you be?"

"OK, Tom, let's look into the underlying issues—"

"Tad."

"What?"

"My name is Tad. You just called me Tom. Go on."

"Tad, people become alienated with things, with people, with the world around them because they have lost touch with what's really important to them. In their lives. What's important to you, Tad?"

"What's important? It's important that I'm important. That's what's important."

"I don't mean superficiality. People become alienated because they've been neglecting key drivers in life, like people, people who matter. Once these personal relationships are addressed, feelings of alienation tend to disappear."

"I don't think that I'm neglecting anyone. Well, maybe somebody.  But I don't think that explains it."

"Could you give me some specifics. I need to know exactly what you've been experiencing."

"Specifics? I don't know. Lots of things. Like restaurants. I went out to eat on Thursday with Laurie, that's my girlfriend, and this law student guy, some recruit, and asked for my steak well done. It comes back medium and when I point it out the waiter apologizes but doesn't bother to take the steak back. I have to ask him to go and cook it some more. People seem to have a hard time following what I'm telling them. I'm always repeating myself. Like they're pretending to listen, you know to be polite, but really could care less. I have to talk very loudly and very slowly like this. And there's other things. Little things. Like nobody calls me anymore. Well, except for a few solicitors. But otherwise nothing. I was buying groceries the other day and the cashier forgot, just forgot, to ask me to pay. She was already ringing up the next customer before I realized what had happened. People don't remember my name. That really bugs me. Like that dinner with Laurie and this hot shot kid they're trying to recruit to her firm from Stanford law. This dinner lasts for I don't know like two and a half hours and we're talking about all kinds of stuff, Hollywood gossip, the hostage situation in Sherman Oaks, which is thinner between linguine and fettuccine. All kinds of stuff. Then I pick up Laurie from her office the next week and I run into this guy again. And he introduces himself to me all over again. Like I wasn't even at the dinner, like I was this beige speck on the wall. Like I'm Mr. Beige all of a sudden. So what do you think about that?"

"I'm sorry. Could you repeat that?"

"What?"

"What you just said."

"What did I just say?"

"About your, problem."

"What problem?"

"The problem, the one that's been bothering you," said Dr. Fellows.

"I remember this place," said Laurie, releasing her hand and placing it over her mouth. "This is where we—"

"Yes, it is," agreed Tad. "I was afraid maybe you had forgotten."

Tad was relieved by her recognition. He had planned everything out. They were standing outside of Rocco's, the small diner where he had first hesitantly asked Laurie's permission for an after-dinner kiss nearly six years ago. It was sunset, which didn't hurt either. Assuming all went well, he had reservations for two at The Palm. He had thought about eating at Rocco's, for sentimental reasons. But, given the way the place had gone downhill, as evidenced by the motorcycles parked outside, he figured The Palm was the safer bet.

"Six years ago today was the most important day in my life," Tad continued. "The day I met you."

"Tad, what are you doing?"

"Something I should have done years ago," he said from his knees. "Laurie, I'm the luckiest man in the world. I don't ever want to lose you. I love you. I've always loved you. Please make me the happiest man in the world. Laurie, will you please marry me?"

"Sure," said Laurie.

"Is that a yes?"

"Yes it's a yes. What do you think I've been waiting for all these years?—Tad? Oh, boy, you're really doing this right," she said, lifting the small light blue box with the white ribbon from his outstretched hands. As Tad scrambled to his feet, she unwrapped the box, revealing the 2 carat diamond ring. After a mild struggle, he managed to get it onto her finger.

"This is beautiful!" said Laurie. Tad gently kissed her. And she kissed back. For the first time in weeks, she kissed back. Tad lifted her up and swung her around—right into a nearby motorcycle. That motorcycle crashed into the next one, which fell into the next, and the next, and the next until five motorcycles lay in a jagged ruin in front of the diner.

"Yow!" he said. Tad hastily let go of Laurie and grabbed her waist. Luckily, no one had seen them. They took a couple of steps towards the car, but not quick enough.

"Where the fuck do you think you're going Blondie?" asked the gentleman, the one with the green Mohawk, leather vest and nipple rings, charging out of the diner.

"That bitch knocked over our bikes," added his heavy-set friend, sporting a goatee and a swastika eyepatch, pounding his right fist into his gloved left.

"Let's teach her some respect!" said another fellow, spittle flying between his two gold teeth. Not one of his 10 remaining associates, piling out of the diner, voiced any opposition to this suggestion.

"Leave her alone!" said Tad. "I knocked over your bikes."

"You did it?" asked the biker with the gold teeth, his eyes squinting.

"Yes me!"

"Now why did you do that for?" he asked, picking up his bike.

"Be more careful next time," added his friend with the green Mohawk. As the bikers tended to their bikes, quite a few voiced similar disapproval: "Klutz!", "Why don't you look where you're going?" "Some people!"

#

Over the ensuing weeks, things progressed nicely. Laurie's friends took notice of her flashy engagement ring and they discussed general timing and locale ideas for the big event, most likely springtime in Big Sur. Holden sent them both a Black and Decker food processor engagement gift and Tad's mother called Laurie at least once a day to plot out bridal gowns and floral arrangement strategies. When Tad and Laurie were alone, however, their relationship followed a detached pattern. Tad's amorous advances were met by friendly cheek pecks and wan smiles. Once he commented that perhaps, after six years together, they needed to "turbo" the intimate part of their relationship and sheepishly displayed a couple of props from his last movie, the one involving renegade nuns and the Spanish Inquisition. But the old spark didn't catch. "Don't worry Tad," she mentioned. "Sex with you is still very fulfilling. Like a nice grilled-cheese sandwich. I really like grilled cheese sandwiches," she added hastily.

First they would get together every other day, then once a week, then once or twice a month, usually for a matinee and some low fat ice creams at Tasty-Freeze. Though the engagement was never officially called off, plannings and discussions slowly petered off. They never fought, with Laurie generally agreeing and nodding to Tad's increasingly shrill monologues, mostly about his search for a new career and the increasingly wide assortment of personal slights to which he fell victim.

As Tad saw his once comfortable bank account dwindle, he began to sell his stock funds, which unfortunately were also diminished by the spate of terrorist acts that were weighing on the market. The Sherman Oaks hostage crisis at this point was entering its fourth month, with no letup in sight. Once the acting assignments disappeared, he pursued a number of other job offerings, but after the first interview, no one had the courtesy to call or write him back.

Tad grew a little stir crazy alone in the apartment for so long and so tended to eat out a lot, at first at fast-food joints and inexpensive diners. People often inadvertently cut in front of him in line and he had to wave his hands to get a waiter to take his order. There were, however, some advantages. Like, if he neglected to stand up, remarking "Check please! Over here, can you bring me my check! I'm finished eating!" waiters forgot to present him with his bill. One time at Bob's Big Boy he got frustrated and walked out without paying. It's their own fault he noted, for this kind of service I shouldn't have to pay. It wasn't just eating establishments. Tad soon found salesmen forgot to ask him to pay for a pair of slacks, a new flatware set, a Samsung 65" TV.

He also could enter freely into trendy nightspots, with the bouncers too distracted to offer objections to his crossing the barrier ropes. Of course, once in the club, he had nothing to do other than avoid getting bumped into by various drunken and high dancers. No one would dance with him, except for once, when as an experiment he dressed in a Bumble-bee jump suit costume with bobbing antennae. He found that if he dressed wilder, he didn't have to yell as much to get people's attention.

There was no mistaking that his birthmark, the one on his shoulder with the odd resemblance to a badminton shuttlecock, was darkening in color. He made numerous trips to dermatologists, but all the tests showed nothing amiss. He was growing tired of spending so many days in waiting rooms trying to get noticed. ("Sir, cymbals are not allowed in the doctor's office.")

He went to the gym, mostly working out in isolation. Sometimes, however, he signed up for tennis. Although Tad's intermediate-level game had not improved, he managed to win almost all his matches, even against highly skilled players from whom in the past he was lucky to win only a few points. His opponents appeared lackadaisical. None of them seemed to care whenever Tad would win points. About the only place he liked to hang out was in libraries, particularly the West LA branch of the public library. He wasn't exactly sure why he liked libraries so much. Perhaps because everyone there was kind of in their own world. Although no one really noticed him, no one really seemed to pay attention to anyone else either. Somehow this eased his isolation. He spent most of his time in the library trying to get some hint as to his condition, either in books and magazines or on-line. He Googled all kinds of things: A.D.D., Alzheimer's, low impact, viruses strange, badminton, nightmares, even philosophy and physics, but there didn't seem to be anything to help him.

After throwing out the clutch on his vintage BMW for the third time, he figured it was time to spring for a new car. After Tad took a new black convertible C series for a spin, the salesman was too busy scouting for other customers to bother inquiring about his test drive. So he drove off with the new car. A few days later while speeding along the 405, he noticed flashing lights behind him.

"Do you realize this is a stolen car?" asked the policeman.

Tad was experiencing a strong head-rush. For the first time in months, someone had initiated a conversation with him.

"Yes, I stole it. I steal lots of things. Stealing is fun!" Tad observed, getting out of the car. He was wearing his favorite striped magenta and lime green jump suit, which he thought helped on the margin in getting some attention.

"It's not correct to steal," admonished the police officer. "You're under arrest."

"I am? That's fantastic!"

Removing a pair of handcuffs, the police officer stated "Please put your hands behind your back."

Tad instead punched the officer in the stomach.

"You should know striking a police officer is illegal," said the officer, upon catching his breath. "I've got things to do. Now please put your hands behind your back."

On the ride to the station Tad kept up a one-way conversation with the police officer, who he now viewed as a life-long friend. He also immensely enjoyed the entire booking and fingerprinting routine, which included numerous procedural questions aimed directly at him with some officers even taking the time to jot down his replies. He did not care for prison food, however, and had to slip out of security quite a few times, usually when the guards were distracted with new prisoners, and take a quick walk across the street to Hardies. Tad was disappointed when on the third day, neither his friend the police officer nor the Mercedes salesman could pick him out of the lineup and he was allowed to go free.

After returning from jail, Tad moped around the house a bit more, occasionally trying to play with Marshmallow who despondently chased a ball a few times before resuming his nap. Tad was making some new friends though, friends with names like Absolut and Jack Daniels. These friends made his days go by quicker. Often Tad would wake up after long sessions with his new friends and not remember what he had done the prior twelve hours. It made him fit in with everyone else who couldn't remember what he did. Tad also spent a lot of time watching TV. *Cops* and *Bad Girls Club* were among his favorites. "Kick her teeth in," Tad heard himself saying to the husband of the woman who had cheated on him with his stepmother. Unfortunately, TV shows were being interrupted quite frequently with terrorist updates and scrolls regarding the ongoing Sherman Oaks Galleria hostage crisis. Once he thought maybe he should escape it all, but it might upset Marshmallow, especially after no one came to feed him or bothered to tend to the results of Tad's handiwork.

The only people he kept in touch with were his mother and Laurie. Sometimes they appeared interested in what he had to say and those times left Tad euphoric. Last Thursday his mother said something interesting when he mentioned his birthmark was annoying him again. "We asked the adoption agency about that mark." Despite the personal contact, he was unhappy that neither his mother nor Laurie initiated any calls to him anymore.

One evening, after a rigorous day of drinking and TV watching, Tad decided to pay a visit to Laurie. They hadn't gotten together in over two weeks and she owed on his count about three phone calls. Jumping the curb across the street with his old BMW, Tad strode to her apartment and banged on the door.

"I hadn't heard from you for a while and I was worried," he said kissing her and walking into the apartment.

Holden was seated at the dining table, which was set for two with a single candle set in the middle.

"Holden, you remember my friend Tad."

"Fiancée, I'm your fiancée Tad."

"Right," agreed Laurie.

"I think Holden was just leaving, isn't that right Holden?" said Tad.

"We haven't had dessert," his ex-agent protested.

Tad grabbed hold of Holden and kicked and punched him out of the apartment.

"This is unfair," Holden said.

"We were just having dinner Tad," said Laurie. "This is so unlike you. You're such a nice guy."

"Oh, now I'm a 'nice guy'? Are you sure?" he questioned. He noticed his right fist was poised in front of her face.

Tad lowered his fist. "Laurie! You've got to stop me!" he said, fiercely embracing her. She did not hug back.

Stumbling out of the apartment, he nearly tripped over Holden and dashed across to the BMW. He didn't make it. Instead he found himself flung into the air, after a brief encounter with the windshield of a late model Buick travelling at 20 mph. He noticed with intellectual detachment that his femur was poking out from the rest of his left leg.

Arriving via ambulance at the emergency room, Tad heard the doctor say, "Shattered femur. Lotta blood loss, O.R.!" A couple of orderlies nodded but then seeing Tad, returned to their other duties. I deserve this, thought Tad. However, that leg was hurting like hell.

"Doctor, take me into the operating room!"

The doctor looked up from the new patient he was examining. "Just a moment sir. This man has a badly sprained thumb. There may be a hairline fracture."

"My leg is fucking broken! Get me to the operating room!"

As he was rolled into the operating room by the expressionless orderlies, Tad had one request for the surgeon. "Just local anesthesia. I want to make sure you finish."

After five days, he released himself from the hospital and took a cab back to his apartment. He had no phone messages. The next four months he spent convalescing at home, tending to his injured leg and eventually sawing off the cast himself. The pain was at times excruciating, but he eschewed any pain killers. His also bid goodbye to alcohol. Tad made a vow never again to allow himself to fall into such a state. He maintained contact with his mother who on occasion would urge him to be more careful after his accident. He also received a get well card, he assumed from the handwriting on the envelope from Laurie although the card itself was unsigned. Throughout these developments, he still watched a lot of TV.

One episode of *The Price is Right* he found particularly riveting. It was the Steeplechase game and a nice retired lady from Midland Texas was up for an all-expense trip for two to "fabulous Toronto!" Just as the cardboard horse was nearing the final hurdle, however, the show was interrupted. Another update from the ongoing Sherman Oaks hostage stand-off, now entering day 182. Yet again, the militants were threatening to kill all eight hostages if their demands were not met. The standoff had begun nearly six months ago when bomb sniffing dogs had foiled the militants' plot to blow up the Sherman Oaks Galleria. While their overall objectives were thwarted, the militants managed to barricade themselves into a store in the mall, Payless Shoes, along with the eight hostages. There they remained for the ensuing 182 days, caught in an odd discount vender Twilight Zone. Food and water were provided daily and the terrorists allowed TV and portable toilets to be brought in. Eventually, a sort of normalcy had entered into the situation, with most of the stores in the mall, excluding Kay-Bee Toys and Orange Julius, which bordered Payless, reopened for business over a month ago. Sales among the other mall stores were up sharply thanks to the endless TV publicity of the ongoing Payless crisis.

Today's bulletin dealt with the terrorists' threat to kill all of the hostages unless the networks provided 30-minutes free airtime to voice their opposition to inmate conditions at Guantanamo along with their revulsion to U.S. fast-food growth in the Middle East. Despite the length of the standoff, there was little doubt the terrorists meant business. All had been prepared to die during the original plot.

Thanks to the bulletin, Tad would never know if the nice lady from Midland would win her dream vacation. "This," said Tad "is pissing me off."

#

After polishing off his bacon cheeseburger in the Galleria Food Court, which he found to be a bit heavy on the sauce, Tad went up the escalator to the barricade area. Given the latest threat, the police and TV camera cordon surrounding the shoe store was particularly active.

"Excuse me!" Tad nudged the nearest officer. "Is that where the hostages are? . . . I said is that where the hostages are!"

"Get back, no one's allowed beyond the blue line."

"OK, I'll just be a minute," said Tad crossing the line and weaving his way through the cement barricades into the store.

"You're not supposed to go in there," observed the officer, reaching to answer his walkie-talkie.

Passing the $5.99 sandals, Tad spotted the eight hostages huddled in the back of the store. He counted ten of the terrorists, three guarding the hostages and seven posted throughout the store aisles.

"Excuse me," Tad asked, tugging on a militant's turban. "Excuse me!"

"What? Who are you? How did you get in here?" the militant answered in halting English.

"I was just wondering if you had these in size 10 ½?" Tad said, indicating the brown loafers he was holding.

"Capitalist pig-dog! I am a member of Jihad Brigade, not a salesman."

"Then what good are you?" Tad responded, punching the militant.

The man recoiled, blood spurting from his nose, drawing the attention of the other six free-ranging militants.

"What's going on?" asked a serious-looking terrorist, who Tad recognized from the TV reports as the ringleader.

"This infidel," replied the injured militant, "just struck me."

"You!" said the ringleader, pointing his AK47 at Tad. "How did you get in here?"

"Those guys," Tad replied, pointing to the three guards minding the hostages, "said today was the last day I could get 2 for 1."

"Did any of you let this infidel in?" said the terrorist turning to the guards, initiating a debate among the terrorists. Meanwhile, Tad untied the hostages.

"Now listen-up!" Tad said to the hostages. "Everyone huddle around me. Come here! Now!" he added.

A silence then a roar went up among the bystanders outside the store as Tad emerged, his arms wrapped around the hostages.

"You'll find the terrorists back in the sneaker section," Tad commented to the chief of police. "They're a little distracted."

"Thanks Mister," replied the chief of police. "You're a real hero," he added before returning to the microphones thrust into his face.

Tad weaved his way past the throng. He wished the Orange Julius was open--the day's activities had made him quite thirsty.

#

"Who is this freelancer? Goes by Mr. Beige?" asked the Deputy Director of Homeland Security.

"He was just here last week to pick up his paycheck. Don't you remember?" asked the CIA's Undersecretary in Charge of Special Operations.

"No, what's he look like?"

"Brownish hair. Or maybe red. Average. I don't know. The important thing is he gets results."

"That's all that I pay attention to," said the Deputy Director.

#

"Mom! It's Tad."

"Tad?"

"Tad! Your son. Your son Tad."

"Oh yes, Tad. How are you doing?"

"Fine. Mom, I have a favor to ask of you."

"Yes?"

"I was wondering if you could take Marshmallow for me. I think he'd be happier with you."

"Marshmallow? I know someone who has a dog named Marshmallow. Nice young man . . ."

#

"I said hi," said the woman, smiling with her appealing metallic grin. Red bobtails flapping, she took five strides towards Tad's favorite chair in the West LA public library and looked down at him.

"What is my name?" she asked quietly. Tad looked at the odd young woman. He glanced at her halter-top which had "ANGELA" scrawled on it in clear block letters. Yes, this top was definitely too tight. He looked back at her face, which was turning a shade of red nearly matching her hair.

"My name!" she repeated.

"Your name? . . . Angela?"

She smiled at this.

"Say it again."

"What? Angela is that right?"

"Again!" she said, a shudder travelling down her body.

"Angela."

"Give it to me!"

"Angela, you're Angela!"

"You bet I am. I'm Angela! This time don't forget," she said shaking her halter-top in front of Tad's nose.

"And you," she said, "are Tad."

"That's right," he said, feeling dizzy. "I'm Tad!"

"Do you mind if I dance Tad?" she added. "I love dancing in libraries." Placing the boombox on top of the reference desk, she turned it on, blasting a song which Tad recognized as the Stones' "Sympathy for the Devil". As she began her dance, a disjointed fusion of jitterbug and capoeira, Tad couldn't help noticing the dark birthmark on her midriff, the one bearing a distinct resemblance to a badminton shuttlecock.

"Please, this is a library," said the reference librarian, before returning to his filing.

# CHAPTER TWO

Angela's library dance was becoming more frenzied, morphing into a Tarantella-Riverdance mix.

"Don't you like to dance?" she asked, her pigtails twirling to the music.

"I uh—"

"Suit yourself," said Angela, nearly toppling an elderly man with a sudden flurry of kicks. "Why are you looking at my breasts?"

"What?" asked Tad.

"You like to look? That's your thing?" she asked, gyrating with her back to him.

"I noticed your birthmark."

"My what?"

"Your birthmark. The shuttlecock."

"What are you talking about?"

"Your birthmark. See look." Rolling up his sleeve, Tad revealed his nearly identical birthmark.

"Cool."

"It's the exact same birthmark!"

"Yeah, isn't it neat?"

"We have the same exact birthmark! Do you realize the odds?" asked Tad.

"It's part of the package."

"What package?"

"What? I can't hear you," she said, doing a poorly executed moonwalk.

"The package. What package are you talking about?"

"You know what makes us the way we are. It's part of the package. Are you sure you don't want to dance?"

"Listen—"

"What are you reading?" she asked.

"This? It's a *Discover* magazine."

"Is it interesting?"

"I don't know. A little."

"You like it more than dancing?"

"This is a library. People read in libraries."

"Are you always this boring?"

"I'm not boring."

Getting up, Tad shuffled his feet in time with the music.

"Dang, look at the time" said Angela, turning off the boombox. "I need to find a rare book, out-of-print."

Fishing out a pair of rhinestone-encrusted eyeglasses, she removed a scrap of paper stuffed in her halter-top. "*From Outhouse to Spa Splurge—The History of the American Bathroom, Second Edition*," she read. "I hope it's not checked out."

"Why is it so important?"

"Who said it was important."

"Strange," Tad said.

"What is? Oh, our birthmarks? That's not all we have in common you know."

"The fact that no one pays much attention to either of us," Tad clarified, pointing to the two librarians and half dozen patrons paying them no attention.

"Besides that."

"We're both bipeds."

"What?"

"I don't know what else we have in common! Maybe we're both Republicans. I don't know."

"You're a Republican?" asked Angela, her eyes narrowing.

"No, not really."

"So you really don't know what else we have in common? You're supposed to be this great secret agent. Mr. Beige, the mysterious man of mystery."

"I never called myself mysterious."

"But you are a secret agent aren't you."

"No, not really. More of an operative."

"An operative. Ooh. Shadowy."

"Look--"

"Red hair," said Angela.

"Huh?"

"We both have red hair."

"OK. So what?"

"Don't you find that kind of bizarre?"

"No not really."

"Only 0.8% of the population has red hair and that's down from an estimated 3.2% 100 years ago. And in another 50 years they estimate there won't be any natural redheads left at all."

"I didn't know that," said Tad.

"And the chances of both of us having red hair. That's like astronomical. It's one of those mathematical progression things. Know what I'm talking about? A factorial . . . 0.8% times 0.8%, that's only a 0.0064% chance that we both have red hair."

"OK."

"That's important. It's a clue. And it will help us find more of us. Other Low-Impactors. Folks who others have a hard time paying attention to."

"There's more like us?"

"Maybe."

"Maybe? Do you know what, who we are?"

"I'd say we're demons."

"Demons? Oh my god!"

"That's just my idea. Maurice thinks we're aliens."

"Who is Maurice?"

"The guy we're going to see. I think demons makes a lot more sense. You know the red hair and all."

"That makes no sense," said Tad.

"OK, then what's your idea?"

"My idea on what?"

"What's your idea on what is causing our condition?"

"I don't know. Maybe some kind of disease. It started for me after I got a cold."

Angela gave off a snorting laugh, her dental gear gleaming. "Like a sneeze? And how does that explain our birthmarks?"

"Maybe it's genetic."

"And our lack of parents. How does it explain that?"

"What?"

"We're both adopted."

"How did you know I was adopted?"

"Maurice told me. And not just adopted but no trace of biological parents either. I was found in a garbage can and you were picked up in front of a hospital right? So you see why Maurice thinks we're aliens. You know, like Clark Kent, left with human parents to bring up. But I don't buy into that. I mean there's no proof at all for UFOs."

"But you think we're devils."

"No, devils are evil. I said demons," said Angela.

"I see."

"Look it beats your idea. Some kind of cold? Even aliens makes more sense than that. How does a disease explain our birth marks? The shadowcocks?"

"Not a shadowcock. Shuttlecock," Tad said rolling up his sleeve and pointing to their birthmarks. "You never heard of a shuttlecock? You know, like in badminton?"

"The thing in *Napoleon Dynamite*?"

"What?"

"The ball? You know with the pole. You punch it," Angela said.

"That's a tetherball. I'm talking about badminton."

"Oh yeah, they play that in South Africa right?"

"South Africa? I don't know, maybe. It's sort of like tennis."

"A shuttlecock you say. Hmm. I always thought it looked more like a moon rover. No, that's not right. Not the rover. Not the thing that landed, not the thing that looks like a bug. The other thing, the thing that goes around the moon but doesn't land."

"The orbiter?"

"Yeah, that's it! The lunar orbiter. Don't you think it kind of looks like that?"

"No it doesn't look anything like a lunar orbiter. It's got like hash marks, see? The orbiter has windows and logos, American flags and so forth. No, it looks just like a shuttlecock."

"Well, maybe you should mention your theory to Maurice."

"Who is this Maurice guy?"

"He's nice. Be sure and compliment his decorating. He's very sensitive on that."

Looking around the library, Angela spotted a pale young man with a lumberjack beard rolling a restacking cart. "Hey, you! Can you tell me where I can find the architecture section?"

The man looked puzzled for a moment, then resumed his reshelving.

"Hey! Grizzly Adams! Where are the architectural books?"

"Excuse me?" asked the man.

"Architecture books. Where can I find them?"

"You're looking for a book?"

"Yes, a book. I notice there are quite a few of them in here. A book on architecture!" she said flicking the man's nose.

"Architecture? Follow me," said the man.

With Tad and Angela in tow, the man suddenly stopped, a puzzled look on his face.

"Architecture books!" Angela repeated.

"Oh right. Yes, those are right here—203.872 through 205.721."

"Thanks," said Angela, poking through the books.

"Here it is!" said Angela, retrieving a small hardcover with masking tape covering its spine. "Let's go."

A middle-aged woman wearing a shirt with RIF— Reading is Fundamental, hesitantly approached them. "Excuse me miss. I'm looking for a book on advanced macramé—"

Punching the woman in the stomach, Angela reached for Tad's hand. "Monitor!"

"What?"

"Monitor! It's a Monitor! She can notice us!"

Tad turned back to the woman who was struggling onto her knees and also pulling out a gun.

"Down!" commanded Angela, fishing out what looked like a toy gun from her knapsack. "Monitor!"

"Here," said Angela, tossing another plastic pistol to Tad. "They pay attention to us. Get it? We *matter* to them" remarked Angela as they crawled their way through the self-help section.

Angela dashed for the emergency exit. With Tad right behind her, they found themselves in an alleyway.

"What car do you drive?" she asked.

"BMW."

"Too slow."

"Go!" said Angela, as they spotted the gun-toting middle-aged woman exiting the library.

Racing down Wilshire, Angela spotted a green Ferrari stopped at a red light. Tossing the man out of the car, she and Tad piled inside.

"Excuse me," remarked the driver.

Five hours later after getting off the interstate, she pulled into the driveway of a mansion. Though hard to determine due to the scaffolding, it could perhaps be best described as a Tudor-Hacienda combo.

"You're late," said a compact bald man with a
freckled face and a shuttlecock shaped birthmark on his neck.
"Here's your book," said Angela, tossing it at him.

# CHAPTER THREE

"I'm Maurice," the man remarked, offering his hand to Tad.

"Tad."

"Or should I call you Mr. Beige?" asked Maurice.

"No, Tad's fine. Really."

"And before that you used to be a movie star? You know you were robbed out of that academy award nomination for *Bloodthirst II*."

"Thanks."

"Did you know we were almost killed trying to get here?" interjected Angela, "Monitors."

"Figures," observed Maurice, "So, up for a tour of the house?" he added swinging his arm around Tad. "You know I'm really glad to see you. I was worried you'd be dead by now."

"Dead?"

"With all your flamboyance and all. Ex-actor, Mr. Beige superspy and so forth. That wouldn't go unnoticed by the Monitors you know," explained Maurice ushering them past some workmen and into the house. "But I'm glad you and your sister made it here in one piece. Let me show you the dining room first. I think it's—"

"Excuse me," said Tad. "Sister?"

"Maurice has it in his head that we're actually brother and sister, biologically. And that we're aliens," said Angela.

"It's obvious," said Maurice. "You both have red hair, you're of similar ages, both put up for adoption about the same time, you both have the lunar orbiter birthmark—"

"Shuttlecock," said Angela. "Tad thinks the birthmark looks more like a badminton shuttlecock than a lunar orbiter."

"Interesting," remarked Maurice.

"Sister?" said Tad. "You think she's my sister? Just because of our hair color and the birthmark? I look nothing like her! This is ridiculous."

"What, because you're a movie star, ex-movie star and I'm not? I'm not good enough to be your sister?"

"What about Maurice? He's got red hair and the same birthmark. Why isn't he your brother?"

"I'm 54 years old," said Maurice. "How can I possibly be her brother?"

"You're 54?" asked Tad surprised.

"I stay out of the sun, try to avoid stress—"

"Agoraphobia, " interjected Angela. "He has agoraphobia."

"I don't have agoraphobia. I just prefer room temperature."

"You're old enough to be our father," Tad said. "Just saying."

"No, I can rule that out," said Maurice. "I've been faithfully married to the same woman for the past thirty-two years and was a virgin before that."

"Then maybe an uncle?" asked Tad.

"Sure, let's go with that," said Maurice, ushering them into the dining room, an oasis of calm compared to the construction commotion going on in the other rooms. The room appeared somewhat stately, almost Victorian, with a long rectangular oak table, high back chairs with ball and claw legs and an oversized chandelier. A number of what appeared to be coconuts adorned the wall, but on closer inspection, they appeared to be small hideous masks.

"They're from New Guinea," said Maurice, beaming.

34

"The craftsmanship is remarkable," said Tad.

"Craftsmanship? These are shrunken heads. Must have been quite a looker in her time don't you think?" he said pointing to one of the faces, with long curly hair.

"About these Monitors," said Tad. "What do they have against us?"

"It's hard to say," said Maurice.

"Maybe they're like us? Do other folks have a hard time noticing them?"

"No, no," said Angela. "They're not like us. They're like the anti-us. Everyone notices them, they're just like regular people you know. The only thing unusual about them is that, unlike everyone else, they notice us. We matter to them."

"But why?" asked Tad.

"Dunno," said Maurice. "We should try and capture one to find out. Don't you think?"

"Maybe you can use your spy skills to trap one of them," said Angela.

"I think Angela has a point," added Maurice. "It's clear they've been aware of you for some time. Else they wouldn't have ambushed you today."

"But why today?"

"All alone you're worth nothing to them," said Maurice. "But once you lead them to Angela, well then they can get to the rest of us."

"In other words, Maurice," explained Angela.

"So there's only three of us?"

"So far," said Maurice. "But we've got another possible candidate. If he pans out, we can put together a team. Then we can begin to fight back. Start taking the initiative."

"The problem is," added Angela, "the Monitors always get the jump on us. They notice us first. It's not fair."

"So, Maurice, is it true you think we're aliens? How does that work?" asked Tad.

"Well, it's just a hypothesis. Actually, however, we're not that much different from everyone else. Just a little more so."

"A little more so what?"

"It's like this," explained Maurice. "Our being aliens, or demons or whatever, is not really all that unique. Sure folks don't pay us any attention unless we put a heck of a lot of effort into it, but really that's just systematic of what's going on all around us. The phenomenon really started thousands of years ago with the founding of Ur. You've heard of Ur haven't you?"

"I can't say I've heard of Ur, no," Tad replied.

"Ur was the first major metropolitan area, the first city, at least in recorded history, somewhere in what is now the Sunni Triangle in Iraq. Prior to Ur, everyone lived in rural areas or small villages. Everyone knew about everyone else. You couldn't just say, walk down the road minding your own business. Everyone knew you. They'd ask you things. How is the harvest going? How're your wives getting along, stuff like that. Everyone knew everyone else. Everyone mattered. Get it?"

"I think so," said Tad.

"But then Ur came around, tens of thousands living in one spot, tradesmen coming from all parts of the world. Well, you see, you couldn't know everyone. For the first time in human history you could become anonymous and it was OK. And it only got worse. Urbanization, the industrial revolution, Jack the Ripper, the Walkman, iPods, Instagram, it's all part of a pattern, get it? Nowadays you see lots of folks walking around with their iPhones, their Bluetooths, not interacting at all with the people around them. Even dating, most of that takes place in cyberspace nowadays. The amount of real personal interaction is at an all-time low. So really we're not all that unique, in many ways we stand at the pinnacle of human evolution. Except of course for us being aliens."

"What about you guys?" asked Tad. "How did you find out about each other?"

"Maurice was doing some research and figured out that I had gotten the Low-Impactor syndrome. He saved me from a Monitor and brought me here to safety, well at least relative safety."

"So is it just the two of you in this giant house?" asked Tad.

"No, my wife Alice lives here too," replied Maurice. "Though we've grown a bit distant. Enough of that though. We've got to focus on the Monitors. They're getting more aggressive you know."

"Yes," agreed Angela. "Now that we're virtually a team, I think we need a name. Teams have names right?"

"The Low-Impactors?" opined Maurice.

"No, that's not nearly as good as the Monitors. We need a cool name like that. . . I've got it. 'The Mysterians', that's cool don't you think."

"Wasn't that a rock band in the 70s?" asked Maurice.

"Don't know, before my time. . . . Oh, wait, I've got it. The Ulteriors! Like ulterior motives…"

"I think you're putting the ox ahead of the cart. Let's get more folks together first before we start worrying about a name."

"But he's got a name," Angela protested, pointing at Tad. "Mr. Beige. See that's cool. I want a cool name too."

"How about Miss Grey?" Tad suggested.

"Miss Grey, yeah I like that!" said Angela.

"Isn't it too close to Jean Grey?" asked Maurice.

"Who?" asked Angela.

"Good point," said Tad. "You know, Jean Grey. X-men? She's the one with the psychic powers, kinda of sidekick to Professor Xavier. You know I was almost cast for the X-men movies. But the fit wasn't quite right."

"Wolverine? You lost out to Hugh Jackman?" asked Angela, her eyes widening.

"No, not the Wolverine. The other guy, with the ray-gun eyes. You know, has to wear those special goggles."

"Cyclops?" asked Maurice.

"Yeah that's the one."

"Oh, I know who you're talking about," added Angela.

"He's the guy Jean Grey goes for isn't he? Except Wolverine also likes her. I could never understand that. Why would she choose this colorless goody-goody, who all he can do is take off his glasses and fire up stuff, when she could have Wolverine. With those claws!" said Angela.

"I don't think he can control the claws—why are we talking about this?" asked Tad.

"Well, the important thing is that we found you and that you're ready to lead us," said Maurice.

"Me?"

"Sure! You're the only one with spy skills," said Maurice.

"What about you. You know a heck of a lot more than I do about all this. You located me and Angela. You should be the leader."

"OK, look. I'll be kind of like Dr. Xavier. But you be the field leader, like Cyclops. Which brings us to our next mission," stated Maurice. "I think I've found another Low-Impactor."

"Oh?" asked Angela.

"He lives in a nursing home."

"A nursing home? How is some guy in a nursing home going to help us?" asked Tad.

"Well, he's not your ordinary nursing home resident. He keeps a very low profile."

"Isn't that typical for people living in a nursing home?" asked Tad.

"He's been in there quite a while. 64 years."

"So what, he's 64 years old?"

"No, he's been in the nursing home for 64 years. A world's record I think. There's other stuff too. Most folks in nursing homes take medications. High blood pressure, heart medicine, diabetes, whatever right? But this guy, just Xanax, nothing else."

"How do you know all this about him?" asked Tad.

"There's a lot of things you can find out on the Internet if you have a lot of time on your hands," mentioned Maurice. "Oh, and one other thing, he's also the longest running contributor to the Republican Party on record. He's given $100 every year since 1932."

"Chet Allen, Sunny Bright Retirement Village, Clearwater Florida," Tad read from the scrap of paper Maurice handed him.

# CHAPTER FOUR

"There's the exit!" said Angela, blowing a bubble and pointing out the green Maybach's passenger window at the sign for San Jose International Airport. Tad wondered how she could manage to blow bubbles while wearing dental headgear.

Maurice furrowed his brow. "I hate the freeway," he said.

Maurice had to get over two lanes, not the usual four Tad had to negotiate when driving to his agent's office in Santa Monica. And there was hardly any traffic. It just goes to show how even simple things become monumental when you remove yourself from society, Tad thought. Despite having a good half mile to move over to the off-ramp, Maurice managed to cut off a red Hyundai Sonata in the process.

"Which airline you guys want" asked Maurice, as they passed the exit for the airport.

"Alaska," said Angela. "I like the Eskimo guy on the plane."

"Terminal C," Maurice said, a bit more relaxed after negotiating his two-lane shift. "Once you land, head straight over to Sunny Bright Retirement Village. And try to keep a low profile."

Tad arched his left eyebrow, the way he was known for in his movies.

"Just in case the Monitors are on the lookout," Maurice added, peering at Tad from the rearview mirror.

"Why would they be on the lookout in a nursing home in Clearwater Florida?" asked Angela.

"They seemed to spot us pretty easily at the library," Tad remarked.

Angela snorted and made another bubble, reminding Tad how much he disliked gum.

"What exactly are we supposed to say to him when we find him?" Tad asked.

"Talk about the weather. That's the number-one subject in nursing homes. And tell him how much you hate Obama," said Maurice, maneuvering the car around an airport shuttle.

"I voted for Obama two times. I think he's great," Tad said.

"I voted for him, too. I mean I would have if I had been registered," Angela said.

"Well, now you're both Republicans. He's been at Sunny Bright for the past sixty years and every four years he sends a check for $100 to the Republican Party."

"Anything else?" Tad asked. At Maurice's blank stare, he added, "On Chet?"

"Yeah, he likes badminton."

"Badminton?" Tad noticed Maurice had a habit of releasing key pieces of information as an afterthought.

"Yes, badminton. In fact, he was once in the top 20 badminton players in the country. In 1951, the year before he entered Sunny Bright, he was ranked 17th."

"17th? How many badminton players are there?" he asked.

"Lots," said Angela. "It's an Olympic sport."

"It is?" asked Tad.

"Well ping-pong and tennis are both in the Olympics, and badminton takes way more skill than they do," said Angela.

"That's true," said Maurice, beeping his horn at the slow-moving Audi convertible ahead of him.

"How does badminton take more skill than ping-pong or tennis?" Tad asked.

"Those two use balls. Badminton uses that thingy, the shuttlecock," Angela replied.

"So any sport that uses a ball is easier? That's your theory?"

"Look at hockey and soccer. Which is harder?"

"Do you think the fact he plays badminton has something to do with our birthmarks?" Tad asked.

"I still think it looks more like a moon orbiter," said Maurice, pulling to the curb in front of the Alaska Airlines sign.

Tad hopped out the back door, eager to stretch his legs. Maurice and Angela had managed to hog all the leg room up front, even though Angela was scarcely five foot.

Maurice popped the trunk, but didn't get out of the car. Hoisting Angela's black duffel bag out of the trunk, Tad was surprised by how heavy it was. He figured by the amount of masking tape she had wrapped around it that she had a habit of overpacking. "What do you have in here?" he asked.

"Just clothes and iced tea," Angela said, exiting the car with her two backpacks she used for carry-on. "Unsweetened. I hear they only have sweet tea in the South."

"OK, guys, have fun!" said Maurice, just before pulling away.

"Drive safe!" said Angela, waving.

Tad gingerly lifted Angela's luggage up by its flimsy handle. "I'll do it!" she said, snatching it from him. Leaning over, she pushed it through the automatic doors while juggling her two backpacks. Tad followed, wheeling in his two suitcases.

Entering the airport, they made their way to the Alaska Airlines ticket counter, or more precisely to the general vicinity of the counter, given the serpentine line in front of it.

"Maybe we should try another airline?" Tad asked.

Kicking her luggage to the front of the line, Angela elbowed past a bespectacled man who was discussing a multi-stop itinerary involving Abilene, Tulsa, and Jacksonville.

"Hey," said the man.

"We need the next flight to Clearwater…Clearwater! Clearwater, Florida!" she said to the slack-jawed gate agent with her hair in a tight bun. "Clearwater!!" Angela repeated, shaking the agent by the lapels.

"Clearwater?" asked the ticket agent.

"Clearwater!" affirmed Angela.

"We don't fly to Clearwater. Closest airport is Orlando."

"OK, two tickets to Orlando!"

"Hey, what about my flight?" asked the businessman.

"Do you see anyone else complaining?" Angela replied, pointing to the other people on line acting unconcerned by the commotion she was making.

"Two tickets to Orlando!" she repeated to the ticket agent.

"You'll have to connect through Seattle," said the ticket agent.

"Fine," said Angela.

"That will be $298 each. The next flight is 3:15."

"There's a flight leaving at 11:02," Tad observed, pointing to the departure board. "Why can't we get on that one? Hey, what about the 11:02 flight!"

"The 11:02? You'll never make that one," said the ticket agent. "Not with security."

"Two tickets, for the 11:02 flight!" barked Angela.

After a bit more back and forth, occasionally jostling the ticket agent as necessary when her attention began to wane, Angela grabbed the boarding passes. Meanwhile Tad filled in the luggage tags for their two largest pieces of luggage. He watched as the mismatched pair went through the baggage carrousel, Angela's piece festively trailing a ribbon of masking tape. By then it was 10:45.

43

Running to the security check-point, they were met by another line, even longer than the one at the ticket counter. Included in the line were a family of Sikhs, a teenage tour group, the usual assortment of businessmen, a matted Irish Setter, and a double wide stroller with twins steered by a sturdy woman.

"We'll never make it," Tad noted.

Angela again jumped to the front of the line, this time shoving aside an elderly woman who was having trouble removing her sneakers. No one seemed to mind. Tossing her backpacks, keys, shoes and cellphone onto the conveyor belt, Angela scooted through the metal detector with Tad following in her wake. The detector went off. Tad started doing a mental checklist as to what it could be. All he had left in his pockets were his medicated ChapStick and the two tissues he always had with him.

"Sir, do you have any metal on you, keys, spare change, a belt buckle..." The belt buckle, Tad thought.

"We don't have the time," interjected Angela, grabbing Tad's hand.

"Sir, you have to go through again," insisted the TSA agent. They continued to collect their items, ignoring her protestations. Tad heard the TSA agent say "Whatever" as they raced off to their gate.

Whenever Tad had to run through an airport, he always envisioned himself as O.J. Simpson in the old Hertz commercials from his childhood. Angela, for her part, was also doing a fair impersonation of the unconvicted double-murderer as she zigged and zagged though the passengers, a backpack dangling from each arm. Why have a backpack if you aren't going to use it, Tad wondered.

After a few minutes of running, he realized he had no idea what their gate number was. Angela seemed to know what she was doing, however, as she dashed through the airport, occasionally batting people with her backpacks. "What's our gate number?" Tad asked.

"23!"

"We are already at 27," he noted.

"A23."

"A23? That's two terminals away!"

"This way," said Angela, running up an escalator marked "Airport Tram."

The tram showed up almost immediately, and three stops later they were let off at the A terminal, arriving at their gate with two minutes to spare. "Now Departing 11:34" read the gate message. Typical, Tad thought.

"You want to get something to eat? I'm starving," Angela stated.

Following her to the airport Wendy's, Tad was surprised that for once she didn't cut in line, probably because they now had time to kill. "We're going Dutch," Angela announced, removing her gum and dental headgear. Tad thought this was a bit inefficient, requiring twice as much repetition of their orders to keep the order taker's attention. Actually the service they received was hardly distinguishable from that of anyone else, as the clerk rarely made eye contact with any of the customers while robotically repeating their orders into the microphone.

As they bit into our hamburgers, Tad couldn't help but notice the marked resemblance Angela had to the girl on the Wendy's bag, although Angela's pig tails were asymmetrical. His musings were interrupted, however, by an Irish Setter, the same one on the security line, gingerly snatching a bacon cheeseburger out of the fingers of a heavyset man wearing an ink-stained muscle shirt. Tad had heard in the old days people actually would get dressed up to fly.

"Bad dog," said the man. Dejectedly, he got back into line, presumably to order another one.

"We are now ready to begin pre-boarding of Flight 882 to Seattle," said the gate agent over the intercom. Wolfing down the remainders of their meal, Angela and Tad jumped to the front of the line and got onboard. Angela plopped into the first window seat she found and tossed her

45

backpacks under their seats. Tad reluctantly placed his carry-on overhead.

"These aren't our seats," he observed, glancing at his boarding pass stub.

"Excuse me," said a huge middle-aged man dressed in cowboy boots and a ten gallon hat, "But I believe you're sitting in my seat."

"Well, I'm here now," explained Angela.

"That's not mannerly," observed the man.

A thirty-something blonde, decked in turquoise and silver jewelry and a black cowboy hat said to the man, "Texy, someone is sitting in my seat."

"Just take these!" said Angela, handing over their boarding passes. Nonplussed, they headed toward the back of the plane.

"Can you get us into Disneyworld?" asked Angela, turning towards Tad.

"What are you talking about?" he asked.

"Disneyworld is in Orlando. If we have some free time, could you get us in for free?"

"How could I do that?"

"Disney? Don't they owe you? All that money you made for them... *The Squid and the Seal--*"

"*The Squid and the Eel,*" Tad corrected.

"You were the Eel, right?"

"That's right. Jonah Hill played the Squid."

"So can you get us in free?"

"We could just walk in. It's not like anyone would care," Tad observed.

"I suppose," said Angela seeming a little dejected. "But I want to make sure it's strictly platonic."

"I'm confused," Tad said.

"Our trip to Disneyworld. I'm not into any of that kinky stuff. All tied up, with your boxers and that ball thing in your mouth," she added.

She was referencing a scene Tad had with Scarlett Johansson in *Catwoman II, Return of the Whip!* Tad recalled fondly Michael Bay required eight takes before he was satisfied.

Not receiving a reply, she continued, "If it makes you feel any better, I wouldn't totally rule out dating you if we weren't siblings. . .And if you weren't so conceited."

"We are not siblings."

"Maurice thinks we are."

"This is from the same guy who thinks our birthmarks look like moon orbiters and that we're aliens."

A peculiar smell appeared, briefly making Tad lose his train of thought. Something like a cross between barbeque sauce and turpentine.

"Well, I think he's wrong about the aliens part. Demons makes a lot more sense to me," said Angela.

"What's that smell?" Tad asked.

"Are you accusing me?"

"No, I was just wondering--"

"Whoever smelt it, dealt it."

Tad noticed at this point that the Irish Setter was lying down in the aisle next to him, with a guilty look on its face. What was it doing on their plane?

"Scram," he said, causing the dog to slink into the back of the plane.

"Hello, folks, this is the captain speaking," came a cowboy voice over the intercom. "There is a slight problem registering with the landing system, most likely just a faulty indicator light. We should be taking off shortly."

Tad gripped the arms of his seat.

"Excuse me!" said a red-faced man sitting in front of them to the flight attendant. "Can we get something to drink? Excuse me? Miss!" But the flight attendant was already scurrying to the rear of the plane.

"Did you notice how the flight attendant totally ignored him?" asked Angela. "Do you think he's like us?"

"He's not like us," Tad replied. "No one gets any attention on airplanes anymore." He closed his eyes.

"What should we talk about?" Angela asked.

"Why do we have to talk about anything?" Tad asked, opening his left eye.

"How about The Invisibles?"

"We don't need a name. There's only two of us, three if you include Maurice," Tad replied wearily.

"Definitely we have to include Maurice. He's like our Professor Xavier."

"Maurice is nothing like Professor Xavier. Professor Xavier controls things from afar with his mind device. Maurice just likes to pontificate from the safety of his house."

"He drove us to the airport," Angela observed. "Well, I still think we should count in Maurice. And if Chet is like us, that's four. Four people is a squad."

"How does four people make a squad?"

"Mod Squad?"

"There were only three in the Mod Squad," Tad said.

"*Charlie's Angels? The A-Team?* We need a name. It builds camaraderie!"

"If you say so."

"How about The Invisibles?"

"We're not exactly invisible. People can see us."

"Well, you know what I mean. ... OK, then. The Low-Impactors."

"What kind of name is that? That doesn't sound cool."

"OK, what's your idea?"

"I don't have one.... The Floaters," said Tad.

"Floaters, where did you get that?"

"You know we kind of just float on by without anyone paying us any attention. Like we're ghosts."

"Then why not just call us the Ghosts? No one would get Floaters. It sounds like an eye disease. I got it, how about The Suaves. That sounds cool."

"Isn't that a type of soap?"

"No, it's a shampoo. Just as good as the big name brands but cheaper."

"I don't think that's exactly the effect we're looking for."

"Our enemies have a name. The Monitors. We need a name too," said Angela. "Something with The in it. All cool names start with The. . .I got it, The Shuttlecocks! That sounds cool. What do you think?"

"It's OK," Tad said.

"Great, that's it then. We're The Shuttlecocks!"

"We've found the source of the problem," said the captain. "One of the indicator lights for the landing system went out. As soon as we get a replacement, we'll be off in a jiffy."

Groans were heard throughout the cabin.

"Does this mean we're going to miss our connections?" asked a middle-aged lady sporting blue eyeglasses and white spikey hair, resembling Annie Lennox, seated directly across from them. But the flight attendant had again escaped to the back of the plane.

The captain was back shortly on the intercom, "Good news. They've located a spare indicator light in central maintenance. It's being sent on the next plane from Tulsa."

There was more grumbling about this good news.

"I need a glass of red wine," said the portly businessman seated in front of them.

"Coming right up," said the flight attendant.

"We can get free drinks!" said Angela.

"I'd like a greyhound," Tad replied.

"What's that?" asked Angela.

"Vodka and grapefruit juice."

"Flight attendant! Two greyhounds. Hey, I'm talking to you!"

"Excuse me, did you say something?"

"Yes, we'd like two greyhounds," repeated Angela.

Tad thought that Angela's request hadn't registered, but surprisingly the flight attendant returned in a few minutes with mini-bottles of Ketel One and two half-filled glasses of grapefruit juice. They poured in the contents of the bottles and Angela raised her glass, "To the Shuttlecocks!"

For a few minutes they enjoyed their drinks and Angela didn't say anything. Tad noticed her eyes were closed.

"So, what was your favorite role? I liked you in *Hopalong Cannibal—*" Angela asked, her eyes still closed.

"How about we talk about you," Tad said. "What do you do for a living?"

"Nothing now," she said, a bit defensively.

"OK, how about before. Before you had the problem with the shuttlecock."

"I was in education."

"That sounds interesting," Tad noted, feeling slightly more relaxed after downing the greyhound.

"Actually, the shuttlecock didn't really have much effect on my occupation, not like with yours. The students never paid me much attention anyway."

"Really? With your hair style and the thing you're wearing?" Tad indicated her dental headgear.

"I don't really need the headgear anymore. Helps me get attention. You want another greyhound?"

"Sure, why not?"

"Flight attendant! Darn, where did she go?"

Getting up from her chair, Angela strolled towards the back of the plane. A few minutes later she came back with a fistful of bottles and a carton of grapefruit juice.

After they knocked down the next round, she commented, "Are you feeling tipsy yet?"

"I don't know, maybe."

"Well, don't lose your inhibitions. Just in case we're brother and sister."

"I'd like to just get some sleep," Tad said.

"You know I wasn't just in education. That was my day job."

"Were you also an aspiring actress?" he asked.

Angela shook her head.

"Aspiring dancer?"

"Nope."

"I give up."

"Aspiring waitress."

Tad started laughing, the alcohol getting to him.

"Actually, I started to work as a waitress at Friday's, but I kept getting goofed up on the orders. So they made me into a hostess instead. That was less stressful."

"You were a teacher during the day and a racy hostess at night?"

"You think I'm racy?"

"I was making a joke."

"I do believe you're flirting with me, Mr. Beige."

"No, not really."

"Poking fun at my occupations, at the clothes I wear—"

"I didn't say anything about your clothes," Tad said, glancing at her yellow halter-top with the name "ANGELA!" emblazoned in blue rhinestones.

"Quit looking at my breasts," she said.

Throughout the delay, Tad tried to fall asleep, but Angela would nudge him, occasionally eliciting a few monosyllables in reply.

"Good news, everyone! The spare light has arrived and has already been installed. We're good to go," said the pilot. A chorus of cheers went up in the cabin. At this point they had been on the tarmac for nearly two hours. "We're number eight for departure, so we should be off shortly," he added, cutting short the brief flurry of cheers.

About fifteen minutes into the flight, they were subjected to a series of unnerving jolts. Just as they started to settle down, another one hit and Tad retasted the Wendy's bacon cheeseburger in his throat.

"Folks, we've got a little chop ahead of us," announced the pilot. "So we're going to keep the seatbelt sign on for just a little while longer."

Ahead of us? Tad thought. What about what they just went through? Over the next thirty minutes the "chop" resulted in a terrifying roller-coaster, with their drinks at one point being flung off their trays. Angela, closed her eyes and sang along to her tunes.

The weather gradually subsided, and Tad finally managed to doze off. Upon waking up, he noticed that they were going over the same piece of land again and again.

"Why are we circling?" he asked, trying to disguise the panic in his voice.

"Well, folks," said the pilot, "we're still having a bit of a problem with the landing gear. Most likely it's just the new indicator light, but flight control wants us to be sure."

Cries of alarm went up inside the cabin, and Tad could smell something acrid in the air. Fear.

"So, do you think we should take up badminton?" asked Angela.

"What?" he shouted.

"Badminton. I'm wondering whether it makes sense to take it up."

"I'm wondering whether we're going to crash!"

"You just heard him say it was probably the new indicator light, not the landing stuff."

"Two indicator lights go bad? What's the chance of that?"

"OK, folks," said the pilot. "Please fasten your seat belts. We're going to go in for a landing."

"Did you hear that? Going in for a landing? That's not what they're supposed to say when they're about to land. Can you see the wheels?" Tad asked, jerking his head to the window.

Grabbing his hand, Angela said, "Don't worry, I've been through worse."

"Really?" he asked.

"I was in the Coalinga earthquake. Plaster was coming down from the ceiling."

"Earthquakes don't happen on a plane!"

There was a loud clank, and Tad gasped. He thought they had crashed, but then he saw the runway moving right below them. After a few more seconds, the plane came to a halt, nearly causing Tad whiplash.

"Navy," said Angela.

"What?"

"Navy. The pilot got his training in the Navy, not the Air Force," she observed.

"Welcome to Seattle!" the pilot said cheerily.

Upon deplaning, most of the weary passengers resembled war refugees. Angela, however, appeared no worse for wear. Between the landing gear light delay and the circling, they had missed their connection by over three hours. The Seattle airport appeared deserted, not surprising given it was nearly midnight.

Coming up to the Alaska Airlines Service Center, Angela again went to the head of the line. Some passengers complained, but just a little. Not having people pay you attention sometimes had its advantages, Tad thought.

"We need the next flight to Orlando," Angela informed the service representative.

"That would be 7:35 tomorrow morning. You're also entitled to a $15 voucher for dinner tonight in the food court and a night at the Airport Travelodge."

"Is that $15 each for dinner or combined?" asked Angela.

"Each."

"Excellent and the rooms. We get one room each right?. . .Hey, I'm still talking to you. Do we each get our own room?"

"Yes," replied the agent.

"Excellent."

Given that the food court was closed, they headed to the baggage carousel. Bags were already tumbling out the tunnel and being reunited with their relieved owners.

Angela lurched towards a black duffle bag and hoisting it out of the carousel.

"Thanks," said the spiky-haired lady with the blue eyeglasses, the one who was sitting across from Tad on the plane, as she took her luggage from Angela.

"They all look the same," Angela said, shrugging.

"Yours has tape," Tad reminded her.

Forty-five minutes later, they were the last ones at the carrousel, with no sign of any more luggage, excluding two sorry pieces that kept going around again and again. They headed off to "Lost Baggage," but it was closed. So it was back to the Service Center, where the rep informed them that their baggage would not be available until Orlando.

They made their way outside the airport where the Travelodge shuttle was still in service. "Look, it has a bear!" Angela said, cheered by the logo on the shuttle.

# CHAPTER FIVE

Upon their arrival at the Travelodge, the clerk informed them that they were in luck. There was still one room available (with queen size bed). Making their way back outside, they found their way to the room and Tad unlocked the door. It was stuffy inside and had a brightly-lit red "Exit" sign just inside the doorway.

"I wish this wasn't on the first floor. Anyone off the street can come in here," Angela remarked.

"I'll protect you."

"You're the Riddler, not Batman" she snorted, referencing Tad's prior movie role.

Turning on the light revealed a minimalist non-carpeted room. Tad spotted an old swivel TV mounted on the ceiling in the far left corner. Next to the TV was a sign which said "$1." The bed, which looked to be more of a full than the promised queen, had a contraption which took quarters.

"They charge extra to use the bed?" asked Angela.

"I think it's for vibration," Tad replied. "I haven't seen one of these since I went to Colonial Williamsburg with my parents."

"Vibration? That sounds interesting." After carefully disconnecting her headgear, Angela undid her ponytails and flung herself onto the bed. "Ready!" she said.

Was this the same person, Tad wondered. Without the dental headgear and pigtails, Angela looked like a different person. The fact that she was lying down on a bed enhanced the effect. Recovering, he scrounged out a couple of quarters and plopped them into the machine. The bed immediately hummed to life.

"This is awesome!" Angela purred, her eyes closed. "Come try!"

"I don't think so," he said, but then gingerly lay down next to her. The vibrating massage was better than he had expected, but just as Tad felt his back muscles began to relax, the bed turned itself off.

"Do you have any more change?" asked Angela.

As Tad got up to search, something odd happened. Maybe it had something to do with her auburn hair flowing over the pillow. Or maybe it was her pouty lower lip. Or perhaps it was just Tad's sudden relief from being out of the airplane. Anyway, he moved to kiss her.

The attempt failed, as Angela trampolined off the bed and kicked him in the solar plexus.

"You're getting the couch," she said, in full Ninja position, green eyes blazing. Tad had never noticed the color of her eyes before.

"There is no couch," he observed.

Angela shrugged, causing a tuft of her hair to fall over her left eye.

"I'm not really like this. It was a sudden urge," Tad said.

"Like the ones you had in *Hopalong Cannibal*?"

"No not quite."

"Did you try this same thing with Scarlett Johansson?"

"I already told you, no."

She paused for a moment to bite her lower lip.

"Do you like me more than Scarlett Johansson?" she asked. "You think I'm prettier than Scarlett Johansson?"

"Um—" he said.

"You know if it makes you feel any better, if we weren't brother and sister I might consider going out with you," she said. "But it'd be an extreme long shot, of course."

This, Tad thought was a bit audacious. Two years ago, *People* magazine had ranked him #14 on its "Hottest Bachelors" list, just ahead of the Winklevoss twins, who tied for #15.

"I don't want you to take this the wrong way," he said, "What just happened, it was just an instinctive reaction. On account of the circumstances."

"What circumstances?"

"The plane ride, the danger we were in—"

"What danger? Since when were we in any danger?"

"All I'm trying to say is that in a normal circumstance that wouldn't have happened," he said.

"You're so full of it! I now officially rescind my mercy comment that I would consider going out with you even as an extreme long shot. Just because you were this big shot movie star, The Riddler, Hopalong, you're too good for me?"

"Let's just forget the whole thing OK?"

Sitting down on the bed, Angela began to remove her shoes. "Do you mind?" she asked. As she began to unbutton her dress, Tad finally got the idea and turned around. He heard some rustling which sounded like her getting into bed.

"Can I turn around?" he asked after a few moments. "Yes?"

Not receiving a reply, Tad turned around to see Angela buried under the covers encased by five of the bed's six pillows. Since when he wondered did flophouses like the Airport Travelodge get off providing so many pillows? Next to the bed Angela had left her clothes in a heap, her bra festively topping the formation.

"You sleep in the nude?" Tad asked.

"Pretty much. Sometimes I don't even wear clothes in public," she said.

"I don't believe you."

"Don't tell me you've never tried it," she said.

"I've never tried it."

"Liar," Angela said, tossing Tad the sixth and final pillow. Carefully keeping the sheets around her, she removed a red mask from her backpack and placed it over her head.

Tad turned off the light and quietly stripped down to his boxers. He had a choice of sleeping on the cold, hard floor or moving the two upholstered chairs together. Deciding in favor of the latter, he maneuvered the chairs, making a nails-on-blackboard noise as they scraped the floor.

"You know you're not as buff as you were as the Riddler," Angela said, peering out from her mask at Tad's silhouette from the red glow of the exit sign.

"I thought you were asleep."

"How can I get any sleep with all the racket you're making? What are you doing?"

"I'm making a bed," Tad replied.

"Seriously?" Angela asked, pausing for a moment. "OK, I'll let you in, just no funny stuff."

"I'm not getting in the bed with you," Tad said.

"Why not?"

"You don't have any clothes on."

"Suit yourself," Angela said replacing the mask.

Propping up his pillow on one of the chairs, Tad tried to settle in. Unfortunately, with the chairs right next to each other, the makeshift bed was too short, causing him to sleep in a ball. Getting up, he moved them apart, wincing at the noise. By sleeping on his side, he found he could avoid slipping between the gap.

Just as he was dozing off, however, Tad was awakened by loud and enthusiastic moaning coming from the adjacent room. He realized now why his mother would always refuse a hotel room with a connecting door.

"Ooh baby, yeah do it!" someone said in a gender-neutral voice. Further instructions included, "Not in there!" "That's backwards!" and "Put it on high!"

"Where's the goat?" asked Angela, burying her head under the pillows.

The next morning Tad woke up surprisingly refreshed, noticing the daylight sneaking out below the curtains. The digital clock read 5:25, still plenty of time to get to the airport for their 7:35 flight.

Being careful not to wake Angela, he did a slightly abbreviated version of his usual morning ablutions and slipped back into the previous day's clothes. By this time it was nearly 6:00. Angela had rolled over when Tad was in the shower, but otherwise displayed no obvious signs of life.

Gently, he nudged her. He tried a bit harder which brought a faint smile, but otherwise she still appeared asleep. "Angela?" he inquired, shaking her a bit rougher.

This seemed to do the trick as she removed the red mask and smiled at him, her braces and green eyes sparkling. "Good morning," she said.

Twenty minutes later Angela had completed her morning activities, pigtails and dental headgear in place. As they made their way back to the lobby, Tad noticed many of the same passengers on their original flight milling about. Their vouchers stated that their stay included a "Free Continental Breakfast!" Tad wondered which continent considered burnt coffee, hard circular pastries and do-it-yourself waffles a proper breakfast.

"It's broken," observed the woman with the white hair (now even more heavily gelled and spikey than the previous day) and blue glasses, referring to the waffle machine. Tad was surprised for a moment, but then given all the other people, figured the comment was a general statement.

"These are fantastic," opined Angela, helping herself to a second pastry as Tad quietly ate one of the cloying disks. The airport shuttle pulled up outside, and they piled on, still eating their pastries.

The terminal was bustling when they arrived, a not unexpected contrast to the night before.

"The Eskimo!" exclaimed Angela, spotting the plane parked outside the gate.

Given they were among the last to board, the plane was already mostly full. Pushing past the Irish Setter, Angela found a nearly empty row and claimed the window seat while Tad slipped into the aisle seat next to her. The spikey-haired woman sat down across from him, stowed her luggage and whipped out a Sudoku book. A large businessman seated next to her, was immersed in his iPad. He let out a cheer, echoed by the cheers of *Angry Birds*.

In contrast to the first leg of the journey, the flight took off on schedule. Angela was not in one of her talkative moods and instead was listening to music on her phone.

"Were you bummed you didn't get a nude scene?" asked Angela about a half hour into the flight.

"What?" he asked.

"With Scarlett Johansson," she replied. "You did bondage but no nudity."

"Ah, well, Scarlett requires an extra $100,000—"

Something bumped Tad's tray and he heard a deep bark. The Irish Setter was biting the white-haired woman sitting across from him. Saliva and blood splashed on Tad's arm. The businessman had dropped his game and was saying "Whoa!" A blonde heavy-set flight attendant arrived on the scene, but didn't know what to do. The dog finally released the woman's hand, but continued snarling.

"What happened?" asked the flight attendant, then noticing the woman's injured hand, "Is there a doctor on board?" There were no takers.

At this point a second younger flight attendant arrived carrying a first-aid kit.

"It's rabid!" said the injured woman.

The dog started howling with a crazed look to its eye. Tad briefly considered trying to distract the dog, but remembered reading about how painful rabies shots were.

"This might hurt," said the second flight attendant. As she applied rubbing alcohol to the woman's hand, the woman howled in pain. For a brief moment she and the dog were making identical noises.

"Are you OK?" asked the large businessman.

"Ma'am, please tell me what happened," asked the more senior, blonde flight attendant.

"That dog just bit her!" Tad said, trying to be helpful. No one paid him any attention.

"It bit me!"

"This dog here?" asked the flight attendant, indicating the Irish Setter, who had switched back from howling to snarling. Its black lips were curled up, its crocodilian teeth showing.

"Get it away!" the woman pleaded.

"Is this dog bothering you?" the flight attendant asked. Tad wondered if all the stereotypes about blondes might be true. Couldn't she see the dog was rabid?

"Shoo," said the second flight attendant, ineffectually slapping the dog's rump.

"Shoo?" he asked.

"Maybe it's a service dog," opined the second flight attendant.

"Does this look like a service dog to you? Where's the owner?" Tad asked.

"Does anybody own this dog?" asked the blonde flight attendant.

"Isn't this crazy?" Tad asked Angela.

"He seems OK now," said the blonde flight attendant, this despite the dog's continued growling. "If he causes any more problems, please use your call button," she advised before leaving.

It was at this point that Angela removed her dental head gear and kissed Tad firmly on the lips.

"What was that for?" Tad asked, a few moments later.

"We're not brother and sister!"

"I never thought we were."

"But now we know for sure . . . the dog?"

"Yes? It's crazy."

"What else?"

"It's rabid?"

"Did you notice the color of its hair?" Angela asked. "It's red."

Angela nodded excitedly.

". . . Just like ours," Tad added.

"Yep," she said. "And he's certainly no blood relative!"

"Wait," Tad said, glancing over at the dog, who still had his eye on the terrified woman. "Just because he has red hair doesn't prove he's like us."

"Didn't you think it was odd when we spotted him in the security line off leash all by himself? And then when he stole that man's hamburger? Being on both of our flights with us, all on his own, no owner, no handler?"

"Well, yes, now that you mention it. It is odd. I never really thought about it."

"Neither did I," she said. "Neither did the man with the hamburger. Or the people at the airport, on this plane, security, the flight attendants. No one pays him any attention. No one cares about him. He's like us."

Angela reached across me and scratched the dog's ears. Its growls subsided and it closed its eyes and began to whimper.

"He's like us," Angela repeated softly.

"He's a dog," Tad said. "Where's his shuttlecock?"

"Probably under all that fur." The dog was shaking ever so slightly.

"What's he doing on the plane?" Tad asked.

"That's a good question," said Angela.

"What about her?" Tad asked, indicating the woman with the injured hand. "She certainly notices the dog. You see the dog don't you?" he asked the woman. She blinked once but otherwise remained silent. Tad was starting to feel dizzy.

Angela's eyes widened.

"Monitor," Angela whispered. "Monitor!" she added, pointing at the woman. For a moment Tad stopped breathing. He could feel the blood pounding in his ears.

"You mean like at the library. One of those Monitors?"

Angela nodded.

"Are you a Monitor?" he asked the woman.

"What's this?" asked Angela, indicating a bit of yellow powder on Tad's tray.

"What?" Tad replied.

"Poison! She was trying to poison you. This dog just saved your life."

Tad looked closer at his glass of Coke Zero. A few crystals were clinging to the inside of the glass. The woman was holding her injured left hand, the one she would have reached over to his glass when he wasn't looking.

"Did you put this in my drink?" Tad asked the woman. The dog growled at the woman. "Hey, I'm talking to you!" Tad said. But she did not reply, her eyes remaining fixed on the dog.

"She's faking it," said Angela. "Remember this morning when she told you the waffle machine was broken? She's a Monitor."

The dog began growling again, deeper than before.

"It's not poison! Just a sedative," the woman said.

"Why are you trying to drug me?" Tad asked her. Instead it was Angela who replied.

"Isn't it obvious?"

"No it's not obvious! The dog, the Monitors, us not being brother and sister are obvious to you, but to me not so much."

"She wants to take you hostage. Isn't that right?" Angela added to the woman. "I think we should take her prisoner."

"That will never happen," said the woman.

"There's two of us, make that three, and only one of you," said Angela. The dog placed its head in Tad's lap. "Good dog," said Angela and resumed scratching the dog's ears, as the dog glared at the woman.

63

"What is it boy? Is Timmy in the well?" Tad blurted out. The dog raised its head from his lap and cocked its head at him RCA Victor-like.

"Are you alright?" asked Angela.

"Fine!" Tad said. "I've almost been killed by a Monitor and have been saved by a dog no one notices. You're a Monitor right?" he asked the woman. "What if she has accomplices? You can't tell who's a Monitor! They could be anybody." As he looked around apprehensively, the dog licked his face.

"Not likely," said Angela. "She's the only human who's been with us the entire journey. Besides I bet Big Red here would give us a heads up." The dog returned his head to Tad's lap and Angela resumed her stroking.

"I'll scream," said the woman. "If you try anything, I will scream. I'm not like you, people pay attention to me. *I matter.*"

Angela stopped stroking the dog and it opened its eyes. She got a glazed look, and her nostrils expanded and contracted rapidly. Letting out a howl, she catapulted over Tad, across the aisle and onto the woman. The dog also was trying to get in on the action, barking crazily. At some point the woman's hair came flying off. Unable to get to the woman, the dog instead attacked the wig, shaking it wildly in its teeth. Tuffs of white hair flew about the cabin.

"How can I concentrate with all this?" asked the woman's businessman neighbor, tossing aside his video game.

The woman tried to fight back, but was outmatched. Angela had her hands around the woman's throat.

"What's my name?" she asked the woman.

The woman eyes were bulging out.

"What's my name?" Angela whispered.

"Please, I'm sorry—"

Angela was wearing the same yellow shirt as the day before, clearly marked "ANGELA!" in the purple rhinestones. For a Monitor, Tad thought she was either incredibly nearsighted or perhaps just stupid.

"My name!"

"I don't know, please--" said the woman. "Angela?" asked the woman. Finally she got it, Tad thought.

"Again!" said Angela.

"Angela."

"Louder! I can't hear you."

"Angela! Angela! Your name is Angela!" the woman said.

"All right already," said the businessman.

"That's right," said Angela, gently stroking the woman's cheek. "My name is Angela. And I matter."

With that, she snatched the woman's purse and climbed back into her seat. The dog, meanwhile, let go of the wig remnants and resumed his growling. The businessman returned to his *Angry Birds*. The woman, now revealed to have light brown shoulder length hair, was breathing heavily, glancing from the dog to Angela.

"What were you planning on doing with these?" asked Angela, fishing out two pairs of plastic handcuffs from the woman's purse. "For your boyfriend?"

The woman hardly moved a muscle, except for one, briefly on the left side of her face.

"Millicent?" asked Angela, looking at the woman's driver's license. "Your name is Millicent Fenmoore? And from North Dakota? Is that a real place? I always thought that was added on to even up the flag. Have you ever met someone from North Dakota?" she asked Tad.

"No, I haven't," he replied.

"This is an interesting shade," Angela observed, dabbing on a bit of Millicent's lipstick.

"What about a phone? Check for a phone." Tad said.

"Hold your horses, I was getting to that. Well look what we have here," said Angela, fishing out the phone. "52 contacts? Well I suppose that's a lot for someone in North Dakota. You want to call anybody?" she asked Tad, handing over the phone.

Tad thumbed through the index, whisking past a bunch of names, Best Western, Target, Citibank, Doorman, odd Tad thought given she lived in North Dakota, and then something truly shocking: "Laurie 213-684-2293."

"What is my girlfriend's number doing in here?" he asked Millicent.

"You still have a girlfriend?" asked Angela.

"Ex-girlfriend, she's a lawyer. We were going to be married until the shuttlecock kicked in."

"You mean the chubby one in the *National Enquirer*? I thought you dumped her for Chloe Sevigny."

"Don't believe everything you read," Tad said, suddenly aware how much Angela had been keeping tabs on his personal life. "What are you doing with Laurie's phone number?" he asked Millicent again.

"We were classmates," said Millicent.

"You are too old to be a classmate of Laurie's," Tad said. He had placed her for someone in her 40s, but now with the white wig off, he wasn't too sure.

"Brown, class of 2003," she said.

"Laurie never mentioned a Millicent Fenmoore before," he said. But she had graduated from Brown and the year seemed about right.

"Hello folks," said the pilot on the intercom. "We are nearing our descent to Orlando. We should have you on the ground in just a few minutes."

Tad continued to question Millicent, but all she would only look straight ahead. The plane landed smoothly. "Air Force," announced Angela.

As the plane lined up to the landing gate, the large businessman pushed past Millicent and retrieved his rollaway from the overhead compartment. Other anxious passengers also began getting up and collecting their items.

"The ground crew appears to be on a little break, but we should be able to disembark shortly. Until then please stay seated with your seatbelts securely fastened," said the pilot.

As the passengers began retaking their seats, Millicent made a run for it. She made it a few rows before the dog tackled her.

"Ma'am, I'm going to have to ask you to get back in your seat," said the blonde flight attendant.

"I'm under attack!" said Millicent.

"Yes I can see that, but the captain hasn't turned off the seatbelt sign, signifying it's safe to get up and move about the cabin."

The passengers were getting agitated. "Nutcase," the large businessman whispered to the people seated behind him.

Although people were aware that Millicent was making a ruckus, they couldn't quite grasp the cause. That's because the cause was Angela, Tad and the dog and no one else seemed to mind them one bit. To everyone else Millicent was certifiably insane, like someone hysterical over a houseplant.

Angela crawled over Tad and hoisted Millicent to her feet.

"Flight attendants, prepare for arrival and cross-check," said the pilot, indicating it was OK to leave the cabin.

"What exactly does cross-check mean?" Angela asked Millicent.

"Help!" yelled Millicent, as passengers scurried past her. "Won't somebody please help me?" she pleaded.

"Ma'am, you're free to leave the plane now. Or will I have to call security?" asked the blonde flight attendant.

"Security! Get security! Can't you see I'm being taken prisoner?"

"Ma'am, let's not get excited," said the flight attendant.

At this point, two security men, one bald and one curly, entered the plane.

"I am a lunatic," said Millicent calmly. "Please take me into custody before I hijack a plane."

67

The bald security man pushed her against the bathroom door, while his partner placed her in handcuffs. Millicent was laughing wildly.

"I love hijacking!" Millicent added.

Her gambit was paying off.

As the security men began hustling her off the plane, Tad realized he needed to act quickly. His shuttlecock throbbing, Tad coldcocked the bald one on the side of his head. Meanwhile, the dog lunged for the curly-headed guard, clinging onto the man's arm.

"Ow!" said the bald security officer.

"It's illegal to strike a security officer," observed his curly-haired partner.

"My friend didn't mean it," Angela interjected. "Apologize to the man," she instructed Tad.

"I'm sorry," he said. "This woman is with us. We can take it from here."

"Don't let them! Arrest me! Arrest me!" yelled Millicent. "I'm a terrorist!"

"Sir, regulations require anyone who appears to be a threat to airport security must be taken into custody," said the bald officer, rubbing his left ear where Tad smacked him.

"Yes I know that. And I sincerely apologize about breaking these important regulations," Tad replied.

The officer paused for a moment, then shrugged. "At least he apologized," he said to his partner. As the security officers exited the cabin, Tad snagged the curly one's handcuff keys.

With Tad on one side of the handcuffed Millicent and the tail-wagging dog on the other, Angela took up the rear, juggling the carry-ons. Millicent continued to complain loudly as they entered the airport. People gave her a wide berth.

"Shuttlecocks rule!" said Angela, fist-pumping, as they entered the baggage claim area. The conveyor belt was already disgorging bags. Rescuing his brown suitcase, Tad noticed Angela's torn suitcase and some Lipton Iced Teas starting to make their way around.

# CHAPTER SIX

Upon securing their luggage, Tad asked Angela whether she had a preference for a rent-a-car.

"Convertible. Red or yellow," she replied.

As the four of them boarded the rent-a-car shuttle, Tad stayed on the lookout for more Monitors. Not that that would have mattered, given Monitors were indistinguishable from anyone else. Forty-five minutes later they drove out of the Thrifty lot in a canary yellow VW EOS convertible. The dog rode shotgun while the luggage, Angela and Millicent scrunched in the back.

"I'm not the enemy," said Millicent, breaking the silence a half hour into the trip to Clearwater.

"Why did you attack us?" asked Angela.

"Trying to drug you isn't exactly an attack. I was the one who was attacked."

"OK, why drug me?" Tad asked.

"I wanted to capture you . . . for interrogation."

"So you knew Tad's ex-girlfriend?" Angela asked.

"I'll ask those questions," Tad interjected.

"You sure you want to hear this?" asked Millicent.

"Out with it, Monitor!" Angela said.

"Laurie, myself and another girl Charlotte were suitemates during our college freshman year," said Millicent. "One day, Char came down with a cold, a pretty nasty one, went to the infirmary. She got better, but something had changed. Laurie stopped talking to her and Char started hanging out with fewer and fewer people. Char thought that she must have said something to set Laurie against her and was also depressed that other people at school no longer wanted to hang out with her. I asked Laurie what was going on with Char. Her answer was 'Who?'"

"Your roommate became a Shuttlecock?" asked Angela.

"A what?" Millicent replied.

"A Shuttlecock. You know someone like us. That's what we call ourselves now."

"Okay...Yes, Char was a Shuttlecock, although at the time I didn't know why I was immune to the effects. One day after biology, I found an ambulance outside our dorm. Sprinting up to our fourth floor suite, I asked Laurie if she had seen Char. 'Maybe on the windowsill,' was her response.

"I dashed back downstairs and banged on the window of the ambulance. The driver was Professor Shapiro from my Psychology 101 class. What was he doing driving an ambulance? He confirmed the worst regarding Char and I went a bit I guess you could say hysterical. He looked at me oddly, then told me to get inside. He quizzed me a bit about how I knew Char, what my feelings were for her and so forth. I thought for a moment that I was under suspicion, but he said not to worry.

"He explained about Char's condition and the reason why I apparently was immune to it. Other people acted sort of autistic in the presence of Low-Impactors, I mean Shuttlecocks, but that we Monitors were immune. He encouraged me to join The Monitor Society, told me how awesome the benefits were, and how people with my ability were hard to come by. It's like we're the antibodies and the Shuttlecocks are the disease."

"I am not diseased!" said Angela.

"Not diseased—A disease," said Millicent. "Anyway, I asked him if he knew all this about Char, why didn't he try to help her? He said it wasn't permitted and that regardless there was nothing that could help her. Most Shuttlecocks only live a short time, succumbing to either suicide or accidents. Since the effect continues after death, it is up to the Monitors to clean up the results."

"How many of us are there?" asked Angela.

"That's classified," said Millicent.

"But the number has been growing in recent years. And now it's apparently spread to dogs. Even more disturbing, Shuttlecocks are starting to notice one another. You guys being a prime example.

"Over the next few weeks, nothing whatsoever happened regarding Char's death. There was no mention of it in the school newspaper, no classmates remembered her, including Laurie. I called up Char's parents myself one day to express my condolences. Her mother acknowledged that Char's death was "too bad" but that was about it. I kept harping on the situation to Laurie and I could feel us drifting apart. After Laurie moved out into a single, I went back to Shapiro and signed up with the Monitors."

"That's a terrible story," said Angela.

"If we all die off so quickly, why don't you just leave us alone. Why try to drug us or kill us?" Tad asked.

"Yes, well," said Millicent. "Most Shuttlecocks die within a few months, but there are some who don't. They strike out in their grief. Two years ago in Luxembourg, a Shuttlecock killed 23 people in a Kate's Paperie with a pair of scissors. No one cared enough about the perpetrator to arrest him. Our only operative in country had to neutralize the Shuttlecock."

"Neutralize, you mean kill?" Tad asked.

"Why not try and help him instead?" asked Angela.

"It's been tried before. Not having anyone else to talk to, Shuttlecocks tend to get a little, a little bit 'clingy' when they meet a Monitor. It never ends well for the Monitor. And then there are some strange cases like Tad, Mr. Beige here."

"What about me?" Tad asked.

"We were on top of the situation with you pretty quickly. Even for Hollywood your career crashed and burned in spectacular fashion. I had remained somewhat friendly with Laurie--Facebook, Christmas cards and so forth. When I started asking how things were going with you, at first she would say 'fine', but over time you faded and I had to remind her that you were her fiancé. When you punched out your agent after he cooked dinner for Laurie, you were pegged for elimination. Display of violence, not good. But then the Payless Shoes thing happened. There had been a few instances in history of Shuttlecocks using their condition for the benefit of others, but never in such showy fashion. I guess you have a flair for the dramatic, given your prior career. So it was decided to resume monitoring you instead."

"But we were ambushed at the library!" Tad said.

"That's right," agreed Angela. "And Tad and I haven't done anything to harm anyone."

"Not everyone agrees on that. A few improvisers tracked you to the library."

"So, are we humans, aliens, demons, or what?" asked Angela.

"You're basically devils," said Millicent.

"I knew it!" exclaimed Angela, "Aliens just never made any sense. Demons are way cooler—Wait, did you say demons or devils?"

"What's the difference?" asked Millicent.

"Demons are amoral, whereas devils are evil," Angela explained.

"OK, maybe it's demons then," said Millicent.

Arriving at the Clearwater exit, Tad pulled into the Sheraton and walked into the lobby.

"Do you have suites?" he asked at the front desk. "Hey!" he repeated, yanking off the clerk's clip-on tie. "Suites? We need a suite."

"Huh?" said the clerk. A few more jostles later, Tad exited the lobby with the key to the "Emperors' Suite." Based on the apostrophe, the suite was magnificent enough for more than one emperor, Tad thought.

The suite was indeed spacious, with a bedroom with two queen beds and a living area with a sofa bed.

"I'll take the sofa," said Millicent.

"That's for the dog," said Angela. "You get the floor."

The one obvious emperor luxury the suite came with was two fluffy robes. Snagging the belt ties, Tad tied up Millicent with two of them, using the same half-Windsor knots he used for his neckties, and stuffed a clean pair of his socks into her mouth.

As they headed out, Tad told the dog to stay, but instead it dashed out the door and started barking.

"What is it boy?" he asked. "Is Timmy in the well?"

"I think he wants to go with us," observed Angela.

As soon as they left, Millicent set to work on undoing her make-shift bindings. . .

Arriving at the Sunny Bright Retirement Village, they set about trying to locate Chet Allen. After struggling to get the lobby clerk to pay them enough attention to answer their questions, they learned that it was the activity period. Mr. Allen could be found either in the TV room (TV-watching constituted an activity), the arts and crafts room (today was macramé), the garden, shuffleboard, the game room, or the meditation room.

They arrived at a door labeled "Meditation Room." Inside they found three women asleep in La-Z-Boy recliners.

"Are they really meditating?" asked Angela.

Wandering down the next corridor, they found the TV room. Some residents were watching Barnaby Jones on a large screen TV.

"Any of you guys Chet Allen?" Tad asked.

"There are no Norwegians in here!" said a man sitting the closest to the TV.

"Is Chet Allen Norwegian?" Angela asked.

"No Norwegians!" affirmed the man.

"Gimme that sweet stuff!" said a resident with huge black glasses, referencing Lee Meriwether on the TV. The woman sitting next to him gave him her elbow.

"This is going to be difficult," Tad observed to Angela.

Next they made their way to the garden, where an employee was assisting the residents in watering the flowers

"Excuse me," Tad asked her. "Is Chet Allen here?"

"Who?"

"Chet Allen? Do you know where he is?"

"Never heard of him."

"He's been living here since 1952," said Angela.

Heading to the shuffleboard, they found a tournament underway, with six teams of two, and an equal amount of cheering spectators. A woman nudged one of the disks out of the scoring area when she figured no one was looking. No one admitted to being Chet Allen.

Returning inside, they discovered the arts and crafts room. No residents were inside, but three nurses were smoking and gossiping. None had heard of Chet Allen.

After wandering down some more corridors, lined with wooden balance rails, they entered the game room. Monopoly, Battleship and cribbage pieces were scattered around the floor, along with Weeki Wachee playing cards and dice.

Inside were two men playing checkers.

"Jump!" said a large man with mutton chops and wearing Burberry wide leg wool trousers.

His skinny partner sat slack-jawed.

"You have to jump. Jump!"

"What seems to be the trouble here?" Tad asked.

"He won't jump!" said the large man with the mutton chops.

At this point, the dog, who had wandered off to sniff something, entered the room.

"Horace!" said the man, his mutton-chops flaring.

"You know this dog?" Angela asked.

74

"Sure, that's Horace."

"Are you Chet?" Tad asked.

"Yes."

"Pleased to make your acquaintance," Tad said, holding out his hand. "I'm Tad Mortriciano."

"Mr. Beige, I know," said Chet, shaking his hand. "What's wrong with your teeth?" Chet asked turning his attention to Angela.

"Oh, you mean the headgear? I use it for effect, so people can notice me a bit easier."

"Were you followed?" asked Chet.

"I don't think so," said Angela.

"What about Millicent?" Tad asked.

"Oh, yeah, we were followed on the plane a little bit," admitted Angela. "We left her in the hotel room."

Chet grunted in acknowledgment and then asked "So can you tell my friend here, he has to jump me?"

"You have to jump in checkers," Tad agreed.

"That's not how I play," said Angela.

"If they just let us play chess, we wouldn't have this problem," Chet said. "But they say we're too senile for chess."

He noticed Tad staring at the shuttlecock on his ankle. "Yes, I have one," Chet said.

"Is it true you've been living in this nursing home for over sixty years," asked Angela.

"I guess so," Chet responded. "The Monitors seem to leave me alone here."

"You're hair doesn't look red," Tad said, observing his salt and pepper hair.

"It is under the roots. I've been dying my hair since my twenties. . ."

"How do you like the weather?" asked Angela, breaking the awkward silence.

"It sucks," said Chet.

"How about those Republicans?" asked Angela.

"Are you a Republican?" replied Chet, inspecting Angela carefully.

"Um—"

"Of course she is," Tad interjected. "We're both Republicans."

Angela, nodded enthusiastically. "I have a signed picture of Newt Gingrich."

Chet harrumphed. "Nowadays, Republicans are nearly as whiney as the Democrats. Giving women the right to vote, that's what started it all. That and the electronic vacuum cleaner."

Angela smiled politely and said, "Well that's certainly a point-of-view."

"I'm sorry, was that rude of me? I guess I'm feeling a little blue, it being Presidents Day and all."

"That's very common I hear over the holidays," said Angela, nodding in agreement. "Do you have any family who comes to visit you?"

"Ha!" said Chet.

"So why do you give $100 to the Republicans every four years?" Tad asked.

Chet shrugged. "I'm a sentimentalist. In my day, Republicans didn't need any help. But now we have to go around begging for votes just like the Democrats. Campaigning. It's undignified."

At this point an incessant buzzing noise went off.

"Fire alarm?" Tad asked.

"No it's time for the evening show and then supper. We'd better get going or Nurse Ratched will come get us."

"Is her name really Nurse Ratched?" asked Angela.

"It's all Nurse Ratcheds here," said Chet.

# CHAPTER SEVEN

As Angela began pushing the wheelchair, the blankets covering Chet's legs slipped to the ground.

"I'm cold," Chet said. Scooping up the blankets, Angela rearranged them, with Chet pointing to the areas where his blue-striped pajamas were still showing. Following the other residents shuffling and wheeling down the yellow hallway, they headed for the entertainment room.

The room was surprisingly large, seating at least 200, and with stadium seating. It was also cold, with the air conditioner grinding in the background. They sat near the back, with Horace jumping onto the seat between Angela and Chet.

As the curtain went up, Tad experienced not one, but two of the things which most appalled him: puppet shows and folk music. The performance featured a snake, played by a white athletic sock; a dinosaur, also a sock, but with white and green felt triangles pasted on for teeth and scales; and a brown starfish played by an actual starfish, though with the need of a visible hand to manipulate it. The snake held the banjo and the starfish played the strings while the dinosaur swayed to the music. The plot involved climate change, safe sex and the healing power of music, although the plot was difficult to follow whenever Horace barked at the puppets. The faint sounds of snoring and wheezing were heard, with the occasional loud snort as someone momentarily awoke.

A half hour later, the dinosaur, suffering from STDs and his habitat destroyed, keeled over, but not before going through a tarantella-like dance of death. A scattering of applause ensued.

"That was powerful," said Angela.

Another buzzer went off, startling Chet awake.

"Where are my blankets?" he asked.

"They're right here," Angela replied.

"Where to now?" Tad asked.

"Dinner," Chet replied, smoothing out the blankets over his wool trousers.

They followed the other residents down the yellow hallway and into the dining room, pausing once for Angela to rearrange the blankets again.

Like the entertainment room, the dining room was also spacious, with gleaming wooden floors smelling of Pine-Sol. Staff members floated by with plates of roast turkey, mashed potatoes, sweet potatoes and peas.

"Is it Thanksgiving?" asked Angela.

"Presidents Day," Chet replied, "We get the same thing every holiday."

Their table went unnoticed by the wait staff. "Be right back," Tad said, heading for the kitchen door.

"Get iced tea, unsweetened!" said Angela.

"Water," said Chet.

Horace barked twice, although it was unclear why.

Securing a large tray, Tad took four fresh plates and some beverages including a bowl of water for Horace. Gingerly avoiding the wait staff and late-arriving residents on his return, Tad handed out the plates and beverages, placing Horace's under the table.

As he reached down for his napkin, Tad found Horace holding the other end, ears back. Tad gave a few strong yanks, but found his chair scraping across the room. Relinquishing the napkin, Tad re-positioned himself at the table.

"Well, Chet," he remarked, "it's good to finally meet you."

"How did you find me?" Chet asked.

"It wasn't easy," Angela answered. "Maurice, he's our leader—"

The mashed potatoes caught in Tad's throat. "He's not our leader," he said.

"Maurice found you on the Internet. He thought being in the same nursing home for 64 years was unusual, and then there was the badminton."

"How did you spot me?" Chet asked, tilting his head 45 degrees at Angela. "How do I know you aren't Monitors?"

Angela slowly raised her shirt exposing the shuttlecock birthmark on her midriff.

"And here's mine," Tad said, revealing the somewhat darker birthmark on his shoulder.

"Yours is quite dark," Chet said, pointing to the lighter colored shuttlecock-shaped birthmark on his own ankle.

"Some days more than others," Tad replied.

"The only Low-Impactor I've ever noticed before is Horace," Chet said, gesticulating with his fork. "Can you pass the ketchup?"

"Maybe it was because we were looking for you to begin with? I also found Tad that way, of course that was pretty easy with all the Mr. Beige stuff."

"Mr. Beige," Chet said. "The guy behind the Payless Shoe rescue."

"Yes, that's me," Tad said, passing the ketchup.

"That's like putting a bulls-eye on your back for the Monitors," Chet said, pounding the ketchup bottle over his potatoes, "What were you thinking?"

"I didn't know about the Monitors then," Tad said.

"And we all keep on paying attention to one another. Amazing."

"Tad still has a pretty hard time paying attention to me," said Angela, dabbing some ketchup onto her mashed potatoes.

"That might not be totally due to the shuttlecock effect," Tad said, musing that Chet and Angela were the only people he noticed who ever put ketchup on mashed potatoes.

"Mmm," said Angela. "I heard you were a pretty good badminton player. Ranked number 17 in the country?"

"I don't do the tournaments. Not anymore," Chet said.

"Because of your legs?" asked Angela.

"No, it's too high profile. You can never be too careful with the Monitors. Why do you think I stay here in Sunny Bright instead of sashaying around all over the place like Mr. Beige?" Chet said.

"I don't think I sashay," Tad said.

"Did you figure anything out about the birthmark from playing badminton?" asked Angela.

"What?" Chet replied.

"Our birthmarks, the shuttlecocks, is there a connection to badminton?"

"Hard to say," Chet said. "Where's the dessert?"

Angela went into the kitchen and returned with three slices of blueberry pie, she thought an odd choice for a nursing home, remembering the old Polident commercials.

"So Chet," Tad said, "You've been living here for 64 years. That's a long time."

Chet shrugged.

"May I ask how old you are?"

"How old?" Chet repeated.

"Yes."

"I can't remember," he said.

"OK, then, what year were you born, do you remember that?" Tad asked.

"1829."

"You mean 1929?" Tad asked.

"I'm pretty sure it was with an 18," Chet said, wolfing down half of his pie in one bite.

"Well if it was 1929, that would make you 84," said Angela. "You don't really look that old."

"According to Maurice, you've been here 64 years," Tad said. "So you were only 20 when you got here?"

"20? No that's not right. I'd say at least 100. What difference does it make?"

"It's a pretty big difference," Tad remarked, remembering the problems his grandmother started having with dates and numbers.

Chet shrugged. "Horace here might be even older than I am," he said. The dog's nose poked out from under the table, covered in potatoes.

"You mean in dog years?" Angela asked.

Chet stared intently at Angela, tilting his head to the right. "Do you think I'm senile?" he asked.

"No, of course not," said Angela.

"What did you use to do before?" Tad asked.

"What is your meaning?" Chet replied.

"What did you do for a living? Before you got here."

"I worked for the government," Chet replied, absently swirling the ice in his water. "Didn't you know that?"

"Maurice only told us about the badminton," Tad said.

Chet tilted his head again. "Do you know my name?" he asked.

"Chet. Chet Allen," Tad replied.

"That's part of the answer," Chet said. "Chet. What's that short for?"

"Charlie?" Tad said.

"No, not Charlie! There is no 't' in Charlie."

"Chartreuse?" guessed Angela.

"It's Chester!"

Chet stared at them expectantly.

"You've got crumbs," observed Angela.

Running his fingers through his facial hair, Chet said "And Allen, perhaps that's not my real last name . . . Maybe it's more like . . . my middle name? . . ."

"Chester Allen Something!" said Angela.

"Republican? . . . Chester Alan . . . Arthur. . ."

"OK," Tad said, filling the silence.

"Chester Alan Arthur! I'm Chester Alan Arthur! . . ."

"Are you related to Bea Arthur?" asked Angela.

"Chester Alan Arthur. President of the United States from 1881-1885," he said. "Also known as the 'Forgotten President.'"

Tad looked at Angela out of the side of his eye and noticed she was doing the same to him.

"Do you like receiving mail?" Chet asked Angela.

"Um, yeah."

"How about you?" Chet asked turning his gaze to Tad. "Do you enjoy mail?"

"Yes I do," Tad said.

"Well you can thank me for that. I signed the Pendleton Civil Service Reform Act into law, even though the Stalwarts fought me every step of the way. What is so appalling is that I was a founding member of the Stalwarts, they were my own faction. Show me a politician nowadays who takes on their own faction. Do you know of any?" he asked Tad, again with a tilt to his head.

"No, of course not," Chet answered himself. "Before the Pendleton Civil Service Reform Act all government promotions were based on nepotism and corruption, the Spoils System. The postal service was run by lazy drunks, not well-dressed professionals. Mail would take weeks to arrive, if at all. I changed all that.

"But about two years after assuming office, I started running into some problems. Some shuttlecock problems, as you two would say. Near the end of my term, even members of Congress couldn't remember who the president was. And then the Monitors showed up. I left office, burned all my personal papers and faked my own death. I travelled the world, pretending to be a wealthy playboy, but they kept tracking me down. Until I finally gave them the slip down here at Sunny Bright . . ."

"That's very . . . interesting," Tad said. He looked out the side of his eyes at Angela again, but this time she was staring intently at Chet.

"You were really elected president?" asked Angela.

"Well, not exactly elected," Chet replied.

"You mean like Bush?" asked Angela.

"No, I never actually ran for president. I was elected the vice-president. I became president after President Garfield was assassinated. His assassin Charles Julius Guiteau said 'I am a Stalwart and Arthur is now president!' right after pulling the trigger."

"You knew him?" asked Angela.

"Guiteau? No of course not! Guiteau was a lunatic. Did you know he was the first person to try the insanity defense? He actually wrote me a letter, asking for a full pardon. Said I owed him because he got me a raise when I became president. Can you imagine?"

"That's ridiculous," said Angela.

"How are you still alive?" asked Tad.

"I'm careful."

"So careful that you live to 184?" Tad asked.

"Low-Impactors don't age," Chet said, snagging an extra slice of blueberry pie from a passing server.

"What?" Tad asked.

"You didn't know that?" asked Chet, digging into the pie. "We don't age, not after the shuttlecock kicks in."

"You mean we're immortal?" asked Angela.

"Immortal?" Chet said, chortling loudly. "Hardly. Low-Impactors die all the time. What with the suicides, accidents, Monitor hitmen and so forth, the average life-expectancy of a new shuttlecock is no more than a couple of weeks. Trust me, we die, and easily.

"But if you're very, very careful, like me, you just might live a long time. Perhaps even as long as Horace. But

83

he takes no chances at all. Spends most of his time sleeping, usually under tables, for added safety."

Tad looked under the table to see Horace still licking his plate, but avoiding the sweet potatoes.

"Biologically I'm 55," Chet continued. "That's when I came down with the shuttlecock."

"You're only 55?" Angela asked. "Do you ever get bored?"

"What do you mean?" asked Chet.

"Being stuck here for all these years in a nursing home? You being an ex-president and all."

"I'm totally off the grid here," Chet said. "The Monitors haven't attacked me since the Ford Administration and I'm not likely to be run over by a car, attacked by wolverines or anything else at Sunny Bright. It's totally safe here."

"So, that's it, just safety?" asked Angela. "That's all that concerns you?"

"There are other things too," he said, a little defensively. "You get over 80 TV channels, the crafts are excellent. Plus, the nurses are smoking."

"I'm not sure it's so safe here," said Angela. "If we could find you, what's to stop the Monitors from doing the same?"

"Monitors have got their hands full trying to keep track of the Low-Impactors they already know about," Chet replied. "They don't have the time or the manpower--"

Lunging from under the table, Horace charged up to an elderly lady in a walker and started biting one of the tennis balls on the bottom of her walker. Paying the dog no attention, the old woman continued her methodical journey to her table.

"Aren't you going to do anything?" Tad asked.

"Like what?" Chet replied.

"I don't know, aren't you his owner?" Tad said.

"I wouldn't say our relationship is exactly like that," replied Chet, finishing up his last piece of pie.

Arriving at her table, the woman shifted out of the walker and into her chair. Horace gave two more barks to the ball and returned back under their table.

"How did the dog get on our airplane?" Tad asked.

"Horace is very resourceful. And even the Monitors have trouble noticing Horace."

"That explains why he was able to ambush Millicent," Angela observed. "And now Horace has joined up with us. You should too!"

"No thanks," said Chet.

"There is power in numbers," Tad said. "If the Monitors find you here, what are you going to do?"

Chet shrugged.

"That doesn't sound like the President Chester—I mean President Arthur I know," said Angela. "The one who courageously signed the Pendleton Civil Service Reform Act. The President Arthur who fought off the Stalwarts? Taking on your own faction! That President Arthur was courageous. He wouldn't be found hiding out in an old folks home. You're so afraid of dying that you're no longer really living," she said, her voice cracking.

Chet's mutton chops drooped. "You're trying to shame me out of leaving Sunny Bright," he said, fiddling with his blankets.

"You said that Horace is risk averse? Then what explains him getting on the plane and saving our lives?" Angela asked.

"Who knows what that dog's thinking," Chet replied. "Besides, what good can I do? No one pays me any attention anymore."

"We pay attention to you," said Angela. "That's a start."

Chet's mutton chops flared. He remained silent for a long time. Then he looked at Angela with his sideways manner. "Have you ever been to Mt. Rushmore?" he asked.

Horace emerged from the table and looked intently at Chet, slowly wagging his tail.

"Not in person," said Angela.

"Do you know who's on it?" Chet asked.

"Lincoln?" she replied.

"That's part of the answer," he said.

"Washington?"

"Yes . . ."

"Grant?" Tad guessed.

"That drunk? Hardly! Jefferson, he somehow managed to get on. But the one who truly annoys me is that fop. The popinjay, Theodore Roosevelt! Do you think Theodore Roosevelt could ever accomplish anything like the Pendleton Civil Service Reform Act?"

"No way!" said Angela.

"I should be on Mount Rushmore, not Roosevelt."

Horace's tail went into overdrive, knocking against Tad's leg.

"Maybe you still can be!" said Angela. "It's a big mountain."

Chet broke down, sobbing, huge gasping sobs. He took out a handkerchief. Then just as suddenly he stopped.

Tossing off the blankets, he lifted himself out of the wheelchair. Tad dropped his spoon. He was huge, at least 6'3" and built like a linebacker.

"I'm Chester Alan Arthur," he said. "And I'm going to win back the presidency."

# CHAPTER EIGHT

T.A. inspected herself in the full-length mirror, adjusting her short-cropped red hair. The birthmark on her midriff, the one which resembled a badminton shuttlecock, appeared somewhat paler than usual. She wondered why this happened on Saturday night football weekends, prior to hitting the Prospect Street eating clubs. Such outings represented the sum total of her Princeton social life, with the rest of her energies focused on her upcoming physics department dissertation defense on dark energy. At the last minute she removed her black pumps in favor of red high heels.

Heading out the graduate dormitory, she retrieved her bicycle from the basement and hopped on for the ten minute ride to Prospect Street. The exercise relaxed her, freeing her mind from reviewing the details of the scandal with her ex-advisor. Over the past six months, she had meticulously removed any possible distractions which could again derail her academic career. She also stopped going by her first name Tiffany, which she regarded as an academic handicap. She now published under T.A. McKenzie.

But tonight was Saturday night on a football weekend, the night where she unleashed some of her own dark energy. She parked her bike at the campus corner of Prospect Street. Today's opponent was West Point and many cadets were mixing into the party scene on the street.

As she stood in front of the first club, Tower, she quickly ruled it out. Too New York. Cap and Gown and Ivy were too preppy. Cottage and Tiger too jock-y. She was going to stick with one of her favorites tonight: Terrace (goths and misfits), DEC (low-key), or Cloister (nerdy). She decided she was in a Cloister mood this evening. Plus, since it was nerdy she didn't feel the need to dumb down her act as much to attract guys.

Walking down the street, she attracted a few long-eyes from the cadets. T.A. absently scratched her birthmark. As she arrived at Cloister Inn, a skinny guy at the door asked her for I.D. When she showed her graduate student I.D., the make-shift bouncer raised an eyebrow but let her pass. Another positive for Cloister was that its uncool reputation made it less picky about who they allowed in.

She heard the cover band playing Blondie, not bad. Avoiding the few students milling about the dance floor, she headed to the basement and grabbed a beer, chugging it in ten gulps, before easing into the second one. Surveying the room, she spotted the undergrads arrayed in bunches. A duo, both sporting close-cropped dark hair and glasses, glanced in her direction. As she walked over, their conversation abruptly stopped.

"Hi fellas," she said.

"Hi, what's your major?" replied the shorter one, wincing nervously. T.A. liked nervous.

"English," she lied. Hearing "Atomic" coming on, she asked "Who wants to dance?"

Leading them both up the stairs to the dance floor, she thought they were hopping too fast for the music. Following the dance, important new information was revealed, as the taller placed his arm around the waist of the other.

"Thanks," she said, silently cursing her bad luck. Heading back down the stairs to the basement, she spotted another undergrad, of average height and sandy blonde hair, standing by himself. He was holding two beers.

"Two beers?" she observed.

"It's for a friend," he said.

"How bout I be your friend tonight?" T.A. asked.

He hesitated for a second. "OK," he said, handing her one of the beers. Another awkward pause ensued with both of them drinking their beers. They went through the "what's your major conversation," with T.A. answering sociology this time. She never responded truthfully, not wanting guys to be scared off by answering with astrophysics. His major was going to be biology, but was most emphatically not pre-med. Nerdy, she thought.

After polishing off their beers, she led him up to the dance floor. While a bit stiff at first, he loosened up a bit as the Pet Shop Boys came on. Must be 80s night, T.A. thought.

"Let's get out of here," she said, as George Michael came on. Grabbing his hand, she picked up the backpack she left in the coat room and led him out of the club. "Your place?" she asked.

Arriving at his dorm room, she removed the gear from her backpack, starting with the ostrich feather.

"I just want you to know, in case, you might have the wrong idea," he said. What was wrong with her luck tonight, she thought. "This is not exactly like, well, it's not something, I've actually done before, I mean not all the way, you know not precisely . . ."

It was actually her lucky night after all. "Put this on," she said, tossing him a red mask from her backpack.

The next morning she woke up a bit groggy and with a sore throat. Her partner was already awake.

"I like your tattoo," he said pointing to her birthmark, which had grown twice as dark as usual. "What is it a moon lander?"

She dressed and gathered her stuff back together, saying she'd be sure to call him. Trudging back to her bike, she rode the ten minutes back to the graduate dorm.

She was definitely feeling more under the weather. She hoped she wasn't coming down with something serious which would interfere with her dissertation defense. As she crossed a street, she was almost run over by a car, the driver oblivious. On the way back to her room, T.A. ran into a couple of fellow graduate students in the hallways. They paid her no attention, despite her disheveled Saturday night attire.

After taking a hot shower and eating a protein bar, she threw herself into her dissertation preparation. Given the fallout from the scandal with her ex-advisor, the administration gave her permission to seek publication under her own name, not under that of her advisor. Her new advisor was the only female full-professor in the department, Sally Pemberton. Pemberton's work focused on the Oort Cloud, the outskirts of the solar system containing Pluto and other dwarf planets. T.A.'s specialty dealt with the more esoteric topic of dark energy, the mysterious fifth energy source which was indirectly discovered in supernovae observations in late 1990s.

T.A.'s first advisor was Calvin Morrison, who at age forty-two was the leading grant recipient of Princeton's physics department, thanks to his celebrity status as co-host of a Discovery Channel mini-series. His work suggested a link between dark energy and "quiescence," Einstein's once discredited cosmological constant. T.A.'s work went beyond this, mathematically linking dark energy with dark matter, in much the same way Einstein linked energy and visible matter.

At first T.A. was excited to be working under the charismatic Dr. Morrison, who took an unusual interest in both her work and her personal life. T.A. found herself in an increasing torrid relationship with her charismatic advisor. Having grown up in foster homes--she was found at four months of age in the waste paper basket of a Sunoco station—T.A. had little experience with interpersonal relationships. Only the third of her five foster mothers took an interest in her, the others focused more on maximizing the funding which came with her case. This one caring foster mother, the one who called T.A. "her angel", died in an automobile accident when T.A. was seven.

T.A. was shocked when she found her work lifted in its entirety in the scientific journal Nature, but published under her advisor's name without so much as an acknowledgement of her own input. She complained, but the interdepartmental hearing sided with Morrison. T.A. retaliated by threatening to post a video on RedTube of herself and Morrison under the Atlantic City Boardwalk, a mutually assured destruction for the both of them. The scandal was swept under the carpet and she was assigned Dr. Pemberton as her new advisor.

Over the next few days, T.A.'s cold continued to get worse. She tried to combat it with a NyQuil/Red Bull cocktail. Still she found her concentration lacking, particularly when parsing her mathematical modelling. Einstein, in the greatest embarrassment to his career, once made a garish mathematical mistake, which was discovered in subsequent peer review. Einstein was able to shrug it off, having already made a name for himself with some work he did in a patent office, called the Theory of Special Relativity. T.A. would not be afforded such a safety net to fall back on.

She had few distractions preparing for her dissertation given that people were leaving her alone. She figured they were avoiding her due to her illness, but she also was receiving fewer phone calls, emails and texts. Even her two pet rats, Niels and Bohr, which she had rescued from a biology lab, stopped coming out of their cages to greet her.

She was also worried about her birthmark, which was twice its prior darkness and tended to throb and itch. Was it infected? Finally she dragged herself to the campus infirmary. Along the way, somebody nearly a block away was waving wildly at her. It was the blonde guy she had picked up the prior Saturday night.

"Are you stalking me?" she asked.

"A, a little," he stammered, fishing the red mask out of his backpack. "You forgot this."

"Thanks," she said, her face growing as red as her hair.

"I never got your name," he said.

"Penelope," she lied.

"I'm Roger," he said, stiffly thrusting out his hand. "You also left the paraffin wax back at my place."

She found herself inexplicitly drawn to him, perhaps due in part to her isolation over the past ten days. Nevertheless, she started to walk away.

"Can I see you again?" he asked, looking down.

"Maybe," she said breezily, heading across the street. Perhaps after her dissertation defense, but certainly not beforehand. She could have no distractions especially with this awful cold.

T.A. arrived at the infirmary, right ahead of another student.

"How can I help you," the receptionist asked the other student.

After waiting ten minutes in the examination room, T.A. was met by a middle-aged doctor pecking on his tablet. T.A. went through her symptoms, the low-level sore throat, the runny nose, night sweats and her throbbing and darkening birthmark.

"I'm sorry, what was that?" asked the doctor, still pecking.

After T.A. went through her symptoms yet again, the doctor sent her off with an antibiotic prescription and some salve.

Whether from the new medications or just time itself, she overcame her malady over the next few days. However, her birthmark never returned to its lighter coloration. And people still weren't paying her much attention. T.A. relished the lack of interruptions to her dissertation preparation.

One afternoon, she heard a cascading buzzing noise. Her phone, which hadn't rung in over a week.

"Your name is not Penelope," said the voice on the other end. "I found your picture in the physics directory. You're Tiffany McKenzie. I've heard about you."

"I'm coming over," she said.

Arriving at Roger's dorm room, T.A. pulled the shades, turned on the Blue Velvet CD and tossed him the red mask.

"Seven," she said, after he had finished the dance, tossing his briefs back at him. Sheepishly, he put his clothes back on and began again.

"That ranks a nine," she said. "You may proceed."

Afterwards, she found herself wishing to remain with him, whether due to him or just general craving for human contact she couldn't say.

The next day something interesting arrived in the mail. The *Physical Review*, a journal of theoretical physics, had agreed to publish T.A.'s article, essentially a synopsis of her dissertation. Her dissertation defense should be a slam dunk now.

She dialed Roger, feeling the need to celebrate. Over the next few weeks, she was a regular guest at Roger's place. She didn't call him Roger anymore, however, preferring the endearment "Spotty" given his uncanny ability to spot her no matter where she was. He would show up out of nowhere, waving her down outside the graduate dorm, the local WaWa, even inside the hallways of the physics department. Three weeks prior she would have shunned such attention, as an annoyance at best. But instead she found herself drawn to him.

After her publication in the *Physical Review*, T.A. braced for the responses, both in official peer reviews, but also in the hallways of the physics department. But nothing happened. Not even her advisor Professor Pemberton acknowledged T.A.'s coup.

She continued to prepare for her dissertation now only six days away, reviewing her mathematical assumptions and practicing in front of a camera. It was called a "dissertation defense" for a reason—the PhD candidate presents his or her work, during which any of the seven board members could interrupt at any time. Following the presentation, the board members pepper the presenter with questions. T.A. had to anticipate the most likely vectors of attack. She had not really disproven the leading theory, but instead provided a rival theory, a more elegant one mathematically, which also had the advantage of linking dark energy to dark matter for the first time.

At long last, the big day had arrived. Arriving at the physics department conference room, T.A. approached the receptionist.

"Is everyone here?" she asked, but the receptionist didn't look up or reply.

Poking her head into the conference room, T.A. spotted her advisor along with two others, focused on their electronic devices. There were supposed to be seven panelists on the board, where were the missing members? Had they possibly forgotten?

"Um, hello?" she said.

"Go ahead," said Professor Frank Dorchester, the department head.

Whenever T.A. was nervous she tended to speak rapidly and didn't come off as intelligent as she really was. No one interrupted. She explained that to determine definitely whether her thesis was correct would require a particle accelerator even larger than CERN's Large Hadrian Collider in Switzerland to generate the dark energites and dark matterites her theory predicted.

"Finished!" she said when she got to the end, as if she were still in kindergarten when she was the first in the room to completely color in a picture. The panel members should now ask her questions, the "defense" part of the dissertation. Then she would be asked to leave the room while they debated the merits of her candidacy. When reinvited in she would either be greeted by the words "Hello Doctor" or instead with a rejection of the last six years of her professional life.

"Any questions?" she asked.

There were none.

"Should I leave the room?" she asked.

94

"OK," said her advisor Dr. Pemberton.

T.A. waited in the waiting room for what seemed like an eternity. At long last the panelists left together, chatting and saying good night to the receptionist.

"Hello? . . ." asked T.A..

"We'll get back to you," the department chair said. "Just sit tight"

After three days of sitting tight, she walked into the department chair's office and demanded a reply. He was apologetic and said he'd be sure to get to it.

She found some respite whenever she was with Spotty. Alone again in her dorm room, however, the blackness would return. The only emails she received were those which somehow escaped her spam box. No one called her. Every day was like being at the DMV, having to repeat herself two or three times to get someone's attention.

One day at the WaWa, she loaded up an entire basket of groceries, announcing to the clerk and the other customers "I'm going to steal these!" and walked out with no one batting an eye. She took to wearing increasingly bizarre clothing to get noticed, mixing discount clothes with items she stole from Agent Provocateur.

Her dorm room was on the fourth floor. She opened the window and crouched up onto the ledge. Unfortunately, what she visualized was not a clean death but more of a painful mangling, probably leaving her paralyzed, and with no one caring enough to call an ambulance.

Edging away from the windowsill, she called Spotty.

Upon arriving at his room, she stated "So, I walked out of WaWa's with a full basket of groceries without paying, and no one cared. I don't have to pay for anything—all these clothes I'm wearing I stole in full sight. It's like I'm a bug or something. No one cares what I do. I'm really worried I'm not going to be able to control myself. At the WaWa's I seriously visualized stabbing the damn clerk through the chest."

Spotty's eyes widened.

"I need people to notice me, I matter! Violent people matter. People pay attention to them."

"I'm sorry to hear that Tiffany," he said.

"Please don't call me Tiffany," she said, smiling wanly, suddenly conscious of the dental headgear that she had restarted wearing to try and gain attention. "I don't use my first name anymore. Call me Angela, that's my middle name. That's what my mom called me."

"OK, Angela," he said.

"I don't even know why I'm here," Angela said. "I'm just worried that I'm going to do something, something bad either to myself to some innocent person."

"We certainly can't have that," he said, holding a thin string of what appeared to be fishing wire between his hands.

"I'm not in the mood right now," she said.

"We can't allow you to hurt others. I need to protect the innocents—"

As he advanced with the wire, she kicked him and rushed for the door. Recovering his footing, he tackled her from behind. She struggled, getting one of her hands next to her neck, as he tightened the fishing wire.

At that moment, he crumpled to the floor, having been hit over the head by a bottle of Johnny Walker Black held by a portly red haired man covered in freckles and having an unusual shuttlecock-shaped birthmark on his neck.

"I'm Maurice," he said.

# CHAPTER NINE

Grabbing her by the hand, Maurice led Angela down alternating stairwells outside the dorm and across the street.

"Where are we going?" asked Angela.

"To the train station."

"The train station is that way," she pointed at a right angle to where they were running.

"It's safer to go circuitously," he replied.

After weaving in and out of dorms, classroom buildings and Palmer Gymnasium, they made their way to the Princeton train station, where the world's smallest independent train line, the Princeton "Dinky" awaited them, total miles of track 4.2 miles to Princeton Junction. One other waiting passenger, a middle-aged man with hipster hat was seated on the bench engrossed in his cellphone.

"Give me all your money!" Maurice yelled at the man.

"I have a twenty," said Angela.

"I was talking to that guy, making sure he's not a Monitor."

"A Monitor?"

"You know, like your buddy in the dorm room," Maurice replied.

They got onto the train along with the middle-aged hipster. As soon as the remaining passengers left the train, the man removed a pistol and pointed it at them.

"That was a good fake out at the station," said Maurice.

"I thank you," replied the hipster.

The Dinky pulled up to Princeton Junction and the man motioned for them to get up. As they exited the train, a half dozen students jostled in front of them. Seeing an opportunity, Maurice shoved the man and the gun clanged onto the floor and bounced onto the tracks.

"Go!" said Maurice, as he and Angela ran off.

Fifteen minutes later, Maurice finally slowed down to a walk.

"How did you find me?" asked Angela, as they both were still catching their breath.

"It wasn't easy. I was hoping that I was not the only one who was suffering from this, let's call it Low-Impact syndrome, so I did a search, looking for people who were redheads and adopted and suddenly stopped being famous. Your name came up."

"I'm famous?" asked Angela.

"In your field of astrophysics you are, or at least were beginning to be. You were the number two most peer-reviewed astrophysicist in the first half of the year. Even though your dark energy theory was generating strong debate, the peer reviews suddenly stopped. Your theory had not been discredited. It just stopped being mentioned, no one cared anymore."

"Do you think I'm right?" asked Angela.

"About what?"

"About dark energy."

"How should I know?" replied Maurice. "We've got six miles to go to the airport."

"Why are we going to the airport?" asked Angela.

"So we can get to California, that's where I live," he replied.

Two hours later, they arrived at the Princeton Regional Airport.

"You're rich," said Angela, noticing a new model Learjet, the only plane on the runway.

Boarding the plane, Maurice seated himself in the pilot's seat, with Angela buckled in next to him. The plane was well appointed with an office nook, kitchen area, living room with large screen TV and a bathroom with a shower.

Thirty minutes into the flight he remarked, "You are now free to move around the cabin."

Getting up, Maurice went to the kitchen area where he took out a bottle of champagne from the mini-fridge. Opening it with a loud pop, he poured two glasses.

"Should you really be drinking?" asked Angela.

"The autopilot will take care of things until we get into San Jose airspace," he replied.

Angela clinked her glass with his. They gulped down the glasses and Maurice immediately poured two more.

"So," said Angela. "These birthmarks we have. What are they?"

"Good question," said Maurice. "I've had mine examined since I was a kid by various dermatologists, but no one seems to think much of it."

They shared theories of their identities, the link between the darkness of their birthmarks and their condition, the shapes of their birthmarks, and whether they could find a cure. Eventually their excited conversation subsided and they fell asleep.

An alarm woke them a few hours later.

"We're entering San Jose airspace," said Maurice, heading to the cockpit.

After circling the airport once, as they waited for a commuter to land, Maurice took them in for the landing. It wasn't smooth.

"Navy," said Angela.

Guiding the plane off the runway and into a hanger, they exited the plane and walked over to a helicopter which was waiting. Inside was a pilot, listening to some tunes on his phone.

"Watch your head," said Maurice as he entered the helicopter.

"Hey!" he yelled into the pilot's ear, yanking off the earbuds. Maurice took out a wad of one hundred dollar bills and began counting them in front of the pilot. Fifteen bills later, the pilot looked up.

Turning his attention to Angela, Maurice said, "You'd better wear this headset. It gets pretty noisy in here."

Thirty-five minutes later, the helicopter landed in a large grassy area.

"Welcome to Templeton Temple," Maurice announced.

"We're going to a synagogue?" asked Angela.

"Templeton Temple is my home."

"I don't see any house," said Angela.

"It's just a few minutes' walk," said Maurice.

As they entered a wooded area, Angela was startled by loud snorting and then spotted a wild boar running by.

"Hi Snorky," said Maurice to the boar. An ostrich trotted by. "Hello Matilda," he said.

After climbing a small hill, Angela spotting the Versailles-like mansion.

"Templeton?" Angela said. "You're Maurice Templeton, the 3D kingpin?"

Maurice nodded.

As they entered the pool area, Angela spotted a topless middle-aged woman with a young pool boy spreading sunscreen on her voluptuous body.

"Alice, my wife," Maurice explained.

"Modern marriage," Angela remarked.

"She hardly notices me nowadays," said Maurice.

Maurice opened a sliding glass door and they entered into a huge bedroom.

"This is the master bedroom?" asked Angela, marveling at the California king-size bed with huge mirror at the headboard and a Jacuzzi big enough to fit eight.

"Oh heavens no," answered Maurice. "This one's yours."

"Llama," observed Angela as a llama poked its head into the room and wandered back into the hallway.

"The house isn't finished," said Maurice. "I'm always adding on more stuff. I also have my home office and laboratory here. That's where I 3D print my drones. By the way, do you know Tad Mortriciano?"

"The movie star, plays the Riddler? His leotard left little to the imagination," she replied.

"He may be one of us. One day he's the number eight paid actor in Hollywood and then no roles, no mentions in the *National Enquirer*, nothing."

"Isn't that what eventually happens to Hollywood stars?" asked Angela.

"Did I mention he has red hair and was adopted just like you and me? That's not all. Have you ever heard of Mr. Beige?"

"No."

"The Payless Shoes hostage crisis."

"That finally ended didn't it?"

"Yes, thanks to Mr. Beige, aka Tad Mortriciano. Would you like to meet him?" asked Maurice.

"Tad Mortriciano? Me?" asked Angela.

"I think it would be worth a visit. He lives in Santa Monica, though lately he spends most of his time in the Westwood Public Library. You can take the Aston Martin, should take about five hours. But it might not be easy to get his attention."

"Why's that?"

"It took an extreme circumstance for you to finally notice me, your life was in danger. I tried before that, but to no avail."

"I don't remember that."

"Precisely," said Maurice.

"Oh, and you may need this," said Maurice, handing over a plastic gun. "In case of Monitors."

"A toy gun?" asked Angela.

"Not a toy," said Maurice. "It fires real bullets. I printed it here."

"Are you coming with me?" asked Angela.

"It's best if someone keeps track of you and Tad Mortriciano," replied Maurice. "I need to stay here and monitor the drones."

"Convenient," said Angela.

"Oh, one more thing. If you happen to be in the Westwood library, could you pick up a book for me. It's out of print, can't find it online. It's called *From Outhouse to Spa Splurge—The History of the American Bathroom, Second Edition*," Maurice replied.

"Second Edition, got it."

# CHAPTER TEN

"Bookworm!" Maurice Templeton, Founder and CEO of Templeton Printing bellowed into his speakerphone.

Moments later, his CFO Lloyd Crabtree entered the office.

"Where is Fidelity on our road trip? I don't see it on the schedule."

"They will be," said Crabtree. "The bankers are still setting it up."

"And Alliance Capital? I thought we were getting a one-on-one."

"I'll find out," said Crabtree.

"You do that," said Maurice.

As Crabtree beat a hasty retreat, Maurice turned his gaze back on the current issue of *Business Week* magazine, the one with his face on the cover, with the title "Skateboards, Yachts, and Trucks?" As Founder and CEO of Templeton Printing, he had become known as the Henry Ford of yachting for being the first to produce 50-foot yachts affordable to the masses via 3D printing technology.

Like many successful entrepreneurs, Maurice had never graduated from college, dropping out of Northridge Community College in his sophomore year. He started with printing skateboards, which proved to be an instant commercial success. A few years later, he added bicycles, which were even more successful. Then he really hit pay dirt with the 50-foot yachts.

Market research indicated, however, that nearly two-thirds of the printed boats never made it to any body of water, with most used as annexes to houses to impress the neighbors. If he could create 3D printed trucks, he would be able to harness the untapped demand for customers who purchased the boats but did not have the means to tow them into bodies of water.

For the past five years he labored with his engineering staff to create the world's first 3D printed truck. The schematic worked, but he still needed the capital to mass produce it. Hence the new stock offering.

The bankers assured him that the offering would be oversubscribed. Given Maurice's celebrity billionaire status, investors were clamoring to meet him and hear about the stock offering and the new truck. To boost the deal, they needed Maurice on a two-week road trip to meet with institutional investors. Coming with him on the trips would be his CFO as well as the senior investment banking team.

Also accompanying him to the meetings would be Mr. Johnny Walker Black. Maurice once gave an impromptu speech at an investor meet and greet featuring an open bar. He took the whisky bottle with him to the podium, taking swigs for effect. Since then it became part of his public persona.

Maurice enjoyed these investor road shows as they fed his appetite for attention. He noticed that for some reason his light-colored birthmark, which he thought resembled an Apollo moon orbiter, would turn even lighter, nearly white, when he was basking in the glow of investor attention.

As Maurice began reading the *Business Week* article about himself, he nodded in approval. Nerdy kid drops out of community college and revolutionizes transportation with 3D printing. While attending Northridge, he started dating Alice McGuire, who was on the cheerleading squad. Unlike the other cheerleaders, however, Alice had no particular interest in football. She simply enjoyed building human pyramids. She would rather be cheering him on in his intermediate computer programming class, Alice said. Maurice enjoyed Alice's company and he noticed his birthmark would generally grow lighter whenever he was in her presence.

Shortly before dropping out of school to pursue his dream of building the first 3D-printed skateboard, he proposed to Alice, and the two remained happily married for the following twenty-two years. As they grew older Maurice began to appear less nerdy and more distinguished, while Alice grew more voluptuous.

While they did not have children, both he and Alice loved animals, especially exotics. All the animals were free to roam throughout the ramshackle seven bedroom Silicon Valley mansion, even the peccary.

Maurice decided to return home a bit early that day, at 6:00, due to a slight sore throat. He had a surprise with him.

"What's that?" Alice inquired as she greeted him at the door, indicating the package he was carrying.

"Well, I thought in honor of the occasion, I'd get you something special."

"It's not my birthday or Valentine's Day," she said.

"Today is the 11,679th day we've been married."

"11,679th day? What kind of anniversary is that?"

"11,679 is a prime number."

"So?"

"Well unless we both live another 634 years, it is the penultimate prime number anniversary date we will celebrate together."

Maurice would often surprise his wife with gifts for virtually anything, including President's Day, Bastille Day, and one of the Mexican Independence Days.

"What's in the box?" she asked.

"It's chinchilla," he answered.

"You know I don't wear fur."

Maurice opened the box to reveal a live chinchilla, curled up inside.

"Ooh, so soft!" she said, petting it.

After providing the chinchilla with a dirt bath and a bowl of salad, he took Alice out for dinner. However, his sore throat continued to get worse during the dinner.

"Your thingy is darker," she remarked the next morning at breakfast.

"What?"

"You know, your birthmark. The shuttlecock?"

"Oh that. I still think it looks more like a moon orbiter. Yes it is dark."

"You should get it looked at."

"I have. It's just a birthmark."

"Well, promise to take lots of fluids?"

"Of course."

Entering the limo waiting at his house, Maurice made his way to the airport. Sitting next to him in the first class cabin was his CFO Lloyd "Bookworm" Crabtree. The flight attendant was passing up and down the aisles offering drinks to the first class passengers, but didn't acknowledge Maurice, despite his TV appearances.

"May I order a drink?" he asked.

"Sorry, I didn't notice you. What would you like?" the flight attendant replied.

"Johnny Walker Black," he said, his sore throat feeling somewhat better after a good night's sleep.

Her eyes widened, with new found awareness. "Say, are you—"

"Maurice Templeton."

"Oh, I thought Bill Murray."

"This woman thinks I look like Bill Murray," he remarked to Crabtree, as the flight attendant brought the Johnny Walker Black. "What do you think?"

"To be honest, you look a bit more like that other guy, what's his name, the guy who plays the Riddler—"

"Tad Mortriciano? Why, because we both have red hair?"

Arriving in Boston, they were whisked away to a restaurant for a lunch presentation, where they were met by two of the bankers, a capital markets lackey from the investment bank running the road show, and top managers from Fidelity, one of the large institutional investors expected to be clamoring to get into the deal.

Maurice noticed that the portfolio managers seated on either side of him were talking to the person on the other side, leaving him out of the conversation. He was also annoyed that no one had bothered to bring him his signature Johnny Walker Black.

"So, does anyone want to hear about the new truck?" Maurice asked, referencing the main use of funds of the upcoming stock offering. Receiving no reply, he continued, "We noticed from customer satisfaction surveys that only one-third of our customers are actually using our low cost yachts as, well, yachts. Most just have them parked in their back yard for use as an extra bedroom and bathroom or just as status symbols. When we were looking for a logical brand extension, we realized your typical car doesn't have the towing power to get our yachts from the backyards to the boat launches, so we figured trucks—"

"Thanks." interrupted the banker. "I think it's time to order."

The next day as the formal road show began, potential investors' eyes glazed over as he went through his vision for 3D printed trucks. If investors couldn't get excited about what their potential investment funds would be funding, the stock offering would never get off the ground.

"That all sounds very interesting," said one investor from Loomis Sayles, "but what about the costs of creating this new truck. How long do you expect to recoup the investment?"

"Lloyd?" Maurice turned to his CFO.

The rest of the meeting was spent with Crabtree, the investment manager and his analysts reviewing the numbers. The day's other meetings were more of the same.

During the road show week, their trips to Boston, New York, Minneapolis, Los Angeles and London followed the same pattern. Turnout for the meetings was sparse.

"Are you willing to do the deal at $22?" asked the banker on the phone following the road show.

"You said it would price no lower than $28. $22 is not enough, you know that."

Just like that he and his company went from market darlings to pariahs.

"The deal's off," he announced to Alice, who was watching TV back at the house.

"That's nice dear," she said.

"Are you listening to me?" he repeated. "I said the equity offering is off. Do you know what that means?"

"No," she said returning her attention back to *Let's Make a Deal*.

"It means we're in trouble," he said.

When Maurice arrived at work the next day, the conversation for once didn't stop when he walked into the company elevator. He entered Crabtree's office, which occupied the corner opposite his own. The CFO was studying his computer screen.

Maurice glanced at the screen. Templeton's stock was cratering, down 30% at the open.

"All senior officers in the main conference room in five minutes," Maurice bellowed over the intercom.

Ten minutes later he was still the only one in the conference room. Getting up, Maurice went from office to office, physically rounding up his staff and shooing them to the conference room.

"Well, I'm sure you've all heard the equity offering has fallen through. And we have a balloon payment due in less than a month. I'd like to hear possible solutions."

He was greeted by silence except for the head of R&D, who was texting.

"You're fired," said Maurice to the R&D head, who showed no reaction. "Since no one has any ideas, we will have to sell the skateboard and bicycle units to generate cash. Dismissed."

Maurice's problems only accelerated following the meeting. No one would follow up on what he instructed on readying the units for sale.

Then one day, a friendly-looking bespectacled man entered his office with no announcement.

"Who are you?" asked Maurice.

"An investor," said the man. "You've made me a lot of money. I should thank you."

"How did I do that?"

"I shorted your stock. Without a CEO's ability to inspire confidence in investors no project of this scale could get off the ground. And I bet you're having just as much trouble now inspiring your employees."

Maurice listened with incredulity as the man went on to explain Maurice's affliction, that the man himself was what was known as a "Monitor", that Maurice's actions had been under surveillance once it became known among the Monitors that he was a Low-Impactor and that it had to do with his birthmark getting darker.

"I'll have it removed," Maurice said.

"It will grow back," the man replied. "I assume your home life is no better than your work life?"

"I think it's about time you leave my office," said Maurice.

"Certainly, but first I offer a piece of free advice. You should resign the CEO position, and turn the company over to your CFO. It's the best thing for your customers, your employees and your shareholders. It's your fiduciary responsibility."

With that the man let himself out of the office.

When Maurice returned home, neither his wife nor any of the menagerie of exotic animals welcomed him at the door.

"Alice? Are you here dear?" Searching the house he found her in the living room glued to Jeopardy. "There you are. How was your day?" he said.

"You're blocking the TV," she replied.

Turning off the TV, he said, "A man came into my office, an investor. He said it all has to do with my birthmark, that I have some kind of disease or something. When the birthmark grows darker, people don't pay me much attention. Remember when I got sick a few weeks ago and it got darker?"

"Can you tell me later? If Doris wins, she's a Grand Champion, five shows in a row."

A sneeze came from the master bedroom.

"What was that?" he asked.

Walking into the bedroom, Maurice opened the walk in closet. Inside was a naked young man.

"What are you doing here?" asked Maurice.

"Cleaning the pool?"

Maurice punched the man.

"Ow," said Mike, rubbing his broken nose.

Yanking Mike back into the living room, he confronted his wife, who had turned Jeopardy back on. "Do you know this guy?" he asked.

"He's the pool boy."

"The pool boy?"

"We don't have a milkman," she said.

"Get out," he said to Mike, who was already hurrying into his bathing suit.

"Why?" he asked Alice. "Oh, but of course. You don't really care what I think, do you?"

She looked at him blankly.

He headed off to the workshop, where his various devices, primarily 3D printers, were stored. Turning one on, he initiated the program for printing a Smith and Wesson 45 (technically a close approximation cast in plastic). Twenty minutes later it and the plastic, but still lethal, bullets were ready.

Returning to the living room, where his wife was now watching a reality show about a family addicted to collecting patio furniture, he pointed the gun at her.

"You will pay attention to what I'm saying," he said.

She looked at him blankly and then went back to the TV. His hand wavered for a moment and he lowered the gun.

He aimed it at his own temple and pulled the trigger. But the gun jammed.

"Figures," he said.

But, strangely, Maurice actually felt better. Perhaps the gun malfunctioning was a sign. He had still had resources. If anyone could find a way to lick this disease it was him. Until he did so, however, it would indeed prove difficult to continue trying to run his firm in the manner in which he was accustomed.

The next day, Maurice walked into Crabtree's office.

"I am resigning my posts of CEO and President. I will, however, be maintaining my titles of Founder and Chairman, but in a non-executive role. You are now the new CEO and President of the company effective immediately. Did you hear that?" he asked Crabtree. "You're in charge now."

"OK, thanks," said Crabtree, in the midst of reading a text message.

So began the new phase in Maurice's life. He returned home to the same indifference he faced at work. He believed Alice still loved him, it's just that the disease was preventing her from realizing this.

He tried to maintain his old lifestyle as best he could. Handball used to be his favorite sport, but he found his opponents lacking in competitive fire when playing him. Rather than venture outside for exercise, he took to running on a new indoor treadmill that he added to the new wing.

That way he could exercise in his favorite temperature, Room.

Over time Maurice adjusted to his new condition. He stayed more and more inside, sticking to the wing of the house opposite the master bedroom and the male guests his wife took to entertaining. He took more interest in the house itself, adding redundant security systems, decorating, and another wing for a 3D printing workshop, where he started producing 3D drones. He also started getting more relief from Mr. Johnny Walker Black and prescription drugs.

In his absence the company continued to prosper. The truck line was eventually released, thanks to the funds generated by the sale of the skateboard and motorcycle divisions. Because he was the largest shareholder, Maurice's wealth continued to grow.

He also spent a lot of time researching his condition. Dusting off his old textbooks, he purchased a statistics program to help him gain insights on his condition. Perhaps Maurice could find other Low-Impactors like himself. During his rare outings outside he looked for nondescript people perhaps resembling Bob Newhart wandering around.

In his early attempts he searched for famous people who quickly faded away. Milli Vanilli, Dennis Kozlowski, Richard Grasso and Ralph Sampson didn't seem to fit the bill. There were in fact plenty of faded celebrities and sports figures, but that was just part of the usual fast career trajectory for individuals in such fields. What he was looking for was someone who, like himself, went overnight from famous to obscure for no apparent reason.

He did a regression that included independent variables like rich, CEO, famous, egomaniac, loss of popularity/career, moon orbiter, shuttlecock, talented. Basically anything he figured applied to himself that might also hold for others like him. But no one came up who fit the bill.

It was only when he added two new variables, "redhead" and "adopted" to the regression, that something interesting happened. Two names popped up Tad Mortriciano and T.A. McKenzie. The first was an actor who was briefly famous after a few moderately successful movies, *Catwoman II* and *Hopalong Cannibal*, but then disappeared at the height of his popularity. The second was a rising star in the field of astrophysics. McKenzie was published on the subject of dark energy in respected academic journals, unusual for a graduate student, and was referenced by numerous peers. But then the referencing stopped abruptly.

No images of McKenzie came up, but there was a surprising hit with Mortriciano. His face matched that of an individual known as Mr. Beige, who was responsible for the daring Payless Shoe rescue. Why did no one in the media catch this?

Whom should he contact first? Maurice was actually a bit worried about Mortriciano. Surely this shadowy Monitor organization would be aware of Mortriciano. It might be somewhat hazardous to meet him, so he contacted T.A. McKenzie first.

"Hello?" he heard a feminine voice on the other line.

"I'd like to speak to T.A. McKenzie," he said. There was no immediate response. "May I speak to T.A. please? . . ."

"This is she. What do you want?"

He was a bit nonplussed, not having thought of the possibility that T.A. was a woman. "I'm a friend. May I ask, have you been having trouble getting people's attention lately?"

"What?"

"People's attention. Have you noticed it's been getting any harder for you lately? Like a lot harder?"

"Yes, I think it has something to do with my birthmark."

"Your birthmark, what does it look like?"

"Not sure, maybe a moon orbiter or that thingy they use in badminton."

"That's wonderful!" said Maurice. "I mean for me. I have the same problem."

"Nice speaking with you," she said, hanging up.

Maurice realized that he had the same difficulty keeping her attention that he had with other people. This was going to be harder than he thought.

He next called Tad Mortriciano, but the actor was similarly disinterested in what Maurice had to say.

This task would require more direct intervention, beyond what his drones could provide. Maurice figured an astrophysicist would be more of help in unravelling the mystery of their syndrome than an actor, as well as her keeping a lower profile, making her less likely to have garnered the interest of the Monitors.

Taking his jet to Princeton Airport, he took a taxi to the university and found his way to McKenzie in her graduate dormitory room.

Taking a swig from his Johnny Walker Black, he got up the courage to knock on her door. Hearing noises inside, he opened it. Inside there was a struggle going on. So much for McKenzie being the safer choice than Mortriciano. He smashed the bottle of Johnny Walker Black over the assailant's head. This time he kept her attention.

# CHAPTER ELEVEN

"The meeting is called to order," said Larry, the Chairman of the Monitors. "Lexy, could you review the minutes for last month?"

"We decided to go with Coke Zero instead of Diet Coke in the vending machine. The vote was 5-2," said Lexy, the leader of the conservative faction, which favored maintaining the existing protocols when dealing with Low-Impactors.

"Anyone like to second the minutes?"

"I'll second them," said Millicent, leader of the progressive faction, who preferred more intensive actions, regarding Low-Impactors.

"OK, now, what should be done about these Low-Impactors getting together?" asked Larry.

"Maybe it's a good thing," said Lexy. "I feel sorry for them, each one an island. It's no wonder they go crazy."

"You haven't seen them in action together," said Millicent, who had recently escaped being tied up by the Low-Impactors in a Clearwater Ramada Inn.

"And now they have that madman Chester Alan Arthur," added Larry. "Add him to Mr. Beige, the scientist who looks like the Wendy's girl, and the paranoid tycoon. That makes four all together."

"Five. You're forgetting the dog," added Millicent, displaying the bite marks which had almost healed on her wrists.

"Oh yeah, I forgot about the mutt."

"Not a mutt," said Millicent. "It's an Irish Setter."

"You mean like that one?" asked Lexy, pointing to Horace, who was resting under the conference table with his head between his front paws.

"Yes, that's him," said Millicent. "What's it doing here?"

"Can we please maintain focus on the matter at hand?" asked Larry.

#

The Low-Impactor syndrome affected each individual somewhat differently. Chester Alan Arthur had a relatively mild case of the affliction. Usually if he spoke loudly enough and gesticulated with the cane he didn't need, someone would eventually notice him. His condition was also more variable than the others'. Sometimes Arthur's shuttlecock would grow so light in shade that people paid him *more* attention than a normal person. Tad, however, had a bad case of it. He could run naked through a joint session of Congress without anyone bothering to stop him.

But no one had it worse than Horace.

In addition to ceasing to age, other things happened to Horace. His herding instincts grew more powerful and his sense of smell could span a continent. Until recently, Horace was risk averse, spending most of his time sleeping under tables. President Arthur had a similar self-preservation reaction when he chose to live at Sunny Bright Manor Assisted Living. Maurice had also become a recluse, rarely leaving his Silicon Valley mansion. But Tad and Angela, the two newest members, were still not that risk-averse.

Horace was always clever, but either his condition or perhaps just the slow accumulation of experience over the years turned Horace into a veritable canine genius. The dog could follow most conversations, but could only read at a first grade level.

In some ways Horace was smarter than humans, at least in his own mind. Angela overly vocalized when around Tad, unconsciously signaling her receptiveness. But Tad never picked up on this, being both nose-blind and generally obtuse.

And now there was a new danger lurking. Horace sensed that Low-Impactors beginning to pay attention to one another was a symptom of this new larger danger, perhaps a kind of self-preservation mechanism. He could smell that the Monitors were frightened by this new phenomenon. They were converging on the west coast, not far from Maurice's mansion. Horace decided to investigate.

This of course meant travel, something which Horace did not like. In the old days he travelled on foot. But after almost dying from a festering splinter in his paw in the summer of 1848, he started using human methods of transportation. Even post-September 11th, no one cared when they saw Horace trot through airport security or take up an entire row of airplane seats.

At first, Horace had to rely on smell alone to determine whether he was closer to his destination or instead had taken a flight to the other side of the world. Over time, however, he was able to match the names of specific cities on the departure screens with the unique smells of each metropolitan area. He became a capable flyer, even if it took him three or more connections to arrive at his ultimate destination.

The last two years, Horace had split his time between staying with President Arthur in Sunny Bright and with Maurice Templeton in his Silicon Valley mansion. Since both were recluses, Horace was unable to herd the two of them together. Even when actor Tad Mortriciano, aka Mr. Beige, was spotted on TV rescuing the hostages in the Payless Shoe crisis, neither realized that Tad was like themselves and

Horace. Horace barked whenever Tad was on TV, but to no avail.

But when Maurice made a systematic search for other Low-Impactors which led him to learn of Tad, Angela, and Chester Alan Arthur, Horace had decided to help Maurice herd them all together.

#

"What's the big deal about the Low-Impactors getting together? They're not doing anything to hurt anyone," said Lexy.

Millicent again pointed again to the bite marks on her arms.

"You were trying to poison them," said Lexy.

"Drug, not poison," Millicent replied. "I'm not a rogue."

Many at the meeting started speaking at once.

"People with that much natural charisma can be dangerous, particularly when they run countries."

"And the actor. His birthmark was probably white at one time. How else could a guy like that have become a star on the big screen?"

"Mr. Beige? He saved the Payless Shoe hostages."

"One good act doesn't negate 23 mass murders by Low-Impactors and counting. We shouldn't always wait until after they show signs of posing a danger to society before intervening," said Millicent.

Again, everyone began speaking at once.

"23 over 850 years, that's less than three mass murders a century."

"Yes, but now they now they have resources. Maurice Templeton is a billionaire."

"Why are the Low-Impactors starting to notice one another now?"

"What if we bug Templeton's house?" asked Trip, who was blonde and attending his first ever Monitor meeting.

"Tried it. Templeton's place is a fortress. He has it swept for bugs on a daily basis."

"What happens if their shuttlecocks start turning lighter? Doesn't that make it even easier for us to notice them?" asked Trip.

"That's equally dangerous. Do you know how Chester Alan Arthur was before he came down with the condition? He was charismatic. For a while he had the highest approval ratings of any president in modern history."

"Do you think he could re-win the presidency—"

"Technically he never won the presidency, he became president because President Garfield was assassinated."

"Doesn't matter. He can still run for a full term."

"The country survived one Arthur presidency. It can survive another."

"Chester Alan Arthur almost started a war with Mexico, which could easily have spread into a world war. And that was *after* his birthmark turned dark."

"I think you all should see this," said Larry, turning on a video. "It was recorded two days ago."

Chester Alan Arthur was addressing the other occupants in the dining room of Sunny Bright Manor, thrusting his cane at his dinner plate.

"What is this? Meat, fish, Goodyear tire? We demand to know!" he thundered.

The residents started pounding the tables with their silverware, demanding higher quality food. Soon the dining room exploded into a food fight. Octo- and nonagenarians rampaged through the hallways, tossing staff members aside with their walkers.

"Luckily, Arthur's shuttlecock went dark again. But just imagine if it stayed white longer."

"Everyone is getting carried away. Perhaps the condition is beginning to wear off? Low-Impactors start to notice one another, then maybe they start turning back to normal."

"What good does eliminating them do?" asked Lexy. Horace opened an eye. "Who's to say the other Low-Impactors out there, those we don't even know about yet, won't start connecting together?"

There was a brief moment of silence and then the Chairman said, "Let's have the vote. Who is in favor of extracting the Low-Impactor cell?"

"You mean kill them?"

"Yes."

Horace opened his other eye, now fully awake.

Three hands went up, including Trip's.

"OK, all in favor of just continuing our monitoring?"

Three other hands went up.

All eyes went to the tiebreaking vote, the Chairman, Larry.

"Based on the balance of evidence—"

Horace launched himself from under the table and sunk his teeth into Larry's nose. The Chairman gasped and collapsed in a pool of blood. Horace lurched onto the conference table snarling, blood dripping from his jaws.

"Well that was . . . "

"Unfortunate."

"Bad dog," said Trip.

"Is he still alive?" asked Lexy, glancing over at Larry.

"I think he just fainted" said Millicent, "but the vote will have to be postponed."

"Shouldn't we do something about the dog?" asked Trip.

"Let's put it on our agenda for next month's meeting," said Lexy. "All in favor?"

# CHAPTER TWELVE

"The green herringbone? Most certainly not!" said President Chester Alan Arthur, regarding the choice in trousers made by his new personal valet, Max.

The occasion was the signing of the Pendleton Civil Service Reform Act, considered to be the second most important piece of legislation in the country's 107-year history, after the 13th Amendment to the Constitution, which abolished slavery.

Carefully picking his way through his prized collection, which currently numbered 72 pairs of trousers, President Arthur himself selected the narrow-ribbed charcoal herringbone, fashionable, though still sufficiently conservative for the historical moment. All six of the White House press corps, a photographer and over thirty congressmen and other luminaries were expected.

Chester Alan Arthur, the nation's 21th president, was at the peak of his political powers, an American Caesar, dominating the political scene in Washington and, with the possible exception of William Gladstone, the most powerful man in the world. He was a shoe-in for reelection and the newspapers were ablaze with predictions for what the charismatic president had in store for the country.

The Pendleton Civil Service Reform Act was not the only noteworthy political act of Arthur's young presidency. Just a few months previously, he vetoed the Rivers and

Harbor Act, declaring the bill "not for the common defense or general welfare and which do not promote commerce among the States." The pork-laden free-for-all was designed to reduce the national surplus, which, following the Civil War, had grown to the obscene sum of $19 million dollars.

"Why," said Arthur, "if you were to stack each one of these dollar bills, it would reach the height of 1.3 miles!"

Although Congress overrode his veto, Arthur gained widespread support both among the press and the citizenry for his courageous stance. Editorials in the *New York Post*, *Cleveland Plain Dealer* and *Boston Herald* proclaimed him the most influential president since Thomas Jefferson, even ahead of the nation's controversial 16th president, Abraham Lincoln.

Chester Arthur graduated Phi Beta Kappa at age 18 from Union College, where he was president of the debate society. He was an excellent public speaker and he noticed that his peculiar birthmark would often fade in color when he was in front of a lot of people. It was also during his college years that he started dying his hair brown to cover up his natural red, for which his peers would call him "Gingersnaps" as a boy.

As a young lawyer practicing in New York City, Arthur first gained notoriety for prosecuting the government's habeas corpus case against slave-owner Jonathan Lemmon. In another controversial case, he represented the Negro Elizabeth Jennings Graham, who was denied a seat on a New York streetcar. Arthur won both civil rights cases and his victories led to the full integration of all of New York's streetcars.

When the Civil War came, Arthur joined the Union Army. But, instead of getting the combat position he requested, he was appointed to the quartermaster department, where he was eventually promoted to the rank of Quartermaster General. His knack for managing complex organizations, along with Arthur's involvement in the Stalwart wing of the New York Republican Party, led

President Grant in 1871 to appoint him to the post of Collector for the Port of New York.

The position carried an annual salary of $6,500, but factoring in the assessments he received from subordinates as part of the moiety system, Arthur's effective salary was $55,000, a greater sum than that of the U.S. president. It was during this period that Arthur developed his three primary interests in life outside of politics: feasting (partying combined with huge meals), collecting trousers, and fishing. (As a member of the prestigious Restigouche Salmon Club of New York, Arthur once caught an 80 pound bass off the coast of Rhode Island.)

Arthur married and he and his young wife Nell had two eponymous children Arthur Jr. and Nessie. Their third child, William, died in childhood. He also grew out his muttonchops to maximum bushiness and took on the nickname of "Elegant Arthur."

In 1878, seven years after his appointment to Collector, Arthur's gravy train derailed. The new president, Rutherford B. Hayes, was a leading opponent of the Stalwart faction of the Republican Party to which Arthur belonged. He fired Arthur and proposed his position be divided among three of Hayes' political supporters, including Theodore Roosevelt Sr., father of Theodore Roosevelt Jr., who later became president. Arthur, meanwhile, returned to his law practice.

This setback turned out to be a minor one compared to what occurred nine months later. His wife Nell, came down with what appeared to be a bad cold. Within forty-eight hours, she was dead at age 42.

Paralyzed with grief, Arthur spent almost all of his time inside the house, dragging himself into his law office no more than once every two weeks. Arthur's sister Mary Arthur McElroy took on the major role in the family, including raising five-year-old Nell. Chester, Jr. enrolled in Princeton University, eager to escape the pallor which had overtaken the Arthur household.

They say that it takes only three major tragedies for any successful, well-adjusted person to be thrust into insanity, chief among them serious illness and the loss of a job or spouse. Wishing to avoid a third such catastrophe, Arthur spent most of his time in bed.

One day an unexpected guest arrived at the Arthur house.

"Someone wants to speak with you," his sister Mary announced.

"Tell him to go away," Arthur said.

"It's Jim Garfield."

"What! You mean James Garfield?" asked Arthur, propping himself up on his pillows.

"Jim is short for James," she replied.

Wondering what the Republican presidential nominee was doing at his house, Arthur descended the stairs still clad in his pajamas. The mutton-chopped 6'3" Arthur was surprised by Garfield's demure beard and slight stature.

Skipping the usual small talk, Garfield cut to the chase, offering Arthur a spot on the ticket as vice-president. Garfield needed a running mate who could help balance the ticket and Arthur would bring along the Stalwart faction.

Arthur at first refused, stating he had no desire to participate in government.

"That's perfect," replied Garfield. "The vice-presidency has no governing responsibilities whatsoever."

In part because his sister Mary wanted him out of the house, Arthur eventually relented and accepted the offer. The Garfield-Arthur Republican unity ticket won a narrow victory and the Arthurs moved to Washington D.C. As vice-president, Arthur climbed his way out of his depression, and resumed his fishing, trousers and feasting, especially the feasting.

Approximately six months after the election, President Garfield was shot. The would-be assassin Charles J. Guiteau proclaimed himself to be a Stalwart and exclaimed "Now Arthur will be president!" Arthur, who had never met

Gateau, was relieved that the bullet wound missed any internal organs and that Garfield was expected to make a full recovery.

Two months later Garfield was dead, from infection from unsanitary operating instruments, and Arthur became the nation's 21$^{st}$ president. Guiteau requested a full presidential pardon and when Arthur refused, he sued the president for the increased salary Arthur received in becoming president, stating that Arthur would not have gotten such a raise were it not for Guiteau's actions. Guiteau was the first U.S. citizen to try out the insanity defense. He was hanged on June 30, 1882.

As president, Arthur continued to mourn for his wife and commissioned a stained glass picture of Nell at St. John's Episcopal Church, which he could view from his presidential office. Every afternoon he would place flowers on her grave.

Arthur's grief, however, did not prevent him from partaking in the companionship of the opposite sex. Nell would never have wanted the gregarious Arthur to spend the rest of his life alone. Before leaving office Arthur had proposals from three eligible young women. This companionship, while diverting, he placed well below fishing, trousers and feasting.

A few months into Arthur's presidency, a Democratic senator from Ohio, George Hunt Pendleton, proposed the eponymous Pendleton Civil Service Reform Act. The bill aimed to eliminate the role of political favoritism as part of the moiety system in making appointments for the Postal Service and other government agencies. Pendleton instead proposed a meritocracy, including uniform national testing as prerequisites for such appointments. Few believed the bill had any chance of passing, particularly since Arthur himself was a prime beneficiary of the moiety system when he served as the Collector for New York.

Instead, Arthur dashed off a letter to Congress stating his unequivocal support for the Pendleton Civil Service Reform Act. His supporters among the Stalwart faction of the Republican Party were aghast while his democratic opponents, including Senator Pendleton, weren't quite sure how to react. But as the days went on and Arthur began to actively campaign for the reform act, lines of opposition began to wane. As Arthur made speeches, his birthmark would temporarily grow lighter in color.

Because of the sudden swelling of public opinion in favor of the act, it easily passed both houses of Congress. The formal "signing ceremony" was set for the morning of January 16th 1883 in the oval-shaped presidential office.

Arthur did not sleep well the night before the signing, due in part to the onset of a nasty cold. Waking up the next morning, he noticed the birthmark on his left ankle had grown noticeably darker and was throbbing. Given how his wife died from what first appeared to be a cold, Arthur was cautious. Taking a swig of the radium-infused health tonic prescribed by his barber, he set about his morning ablutions.

Arriving in the presidential office, he did not find the rambunctious overflow crowd of press, photographers and politicians he had anticipated. Just two men sitting in chairs chatting with his sister Mary.

"Please tell everyone to come in," he said.

The two reporters looked up and nodded briefly, then went back to their conversation.

"Mary, where are the rest of our guests?" he asked, but she didn't seem to hear him, engrossed in the latest Farmer's Almanac prediction for the winter which one of the reporters was explaining.

"Sister?" asked Arthur, a bit loudly.

The rambunctious dog Horace, who he had adopted a few months ago, let out a bark of surprise.

Mary shrugged. "A photographer was here a bit earlier, but then he left, something about having to photograph the arrival of the Portuguese Ambassador."

"The Portuguese Ambassador? Oh never mind, is this the bill?" he asked, indicating the massive six page document on his desk. Six pages, he thought, that's some bill, must be some kind of record.

After signing the document, Arthur stated "I'm going back to bed." Over the next few days, Arthur stayed mostly to his living quarters, sleeping off the illness.

Instead of front page headlines of Arthur's historic signing of the Pendleton Civil Service Act, with accompanying photographs, there was just a quick story, buried in the back pages.

Feeling better, Arthur decided it was time to schedule a Cabinet meeting to discuss his upcoming agenda. He was still mildly perplexed by the new permanently dark color to his birthmark, but at least it had stopped itching and throbbing. He wondered what was causing the odd malaise, as he put it, which made everyone around him distracted or uninterested.

At least the dog Horace appeared unaffected. He and the dog would take late night constitutionals around town, taking advantage of the unusually mild winter weather they were experiencing. These walks were particularly salutary given that Arthur was not interrupted on the street, and he and the dog would often walk last until the wee hours of the morning. (Arthur was a night owl and rarely retired to bed before 2 a.m.)

On the Cabinet agenda was Arthur's plan to initiate new legislation to aid the plight of the former slaves. He was alarmed by what his Southern Negro friends in Congress were telling him about increased harassment of Negros, including new segregation laws and poll taxes. In addition, the Supreme Court had just struck down the Civil Rights Act of 1875. Arthur expressed outrage at the ruling, but his comments weren't reported in the press.

All seven cabinet members were in attendance: William Windom (Treasury), Frederick Frelinghuysen (State), William Hunt (Navy), Sam Kirkwood (Interior), Timothy Howe (Postmaster General), and Robert Todd Lincoln (War), son of the former president.

Entering the room, Arthur asked, "So, how is the new bill working out?" referring to the Pendleton Act. Horace the dog jumped onto the Cabinet table, but no one raised an eyebrow. Arthur repeated his question more loudly, something he had to do a lot lately.

Timothy Howe, the Postmaster General, replied that 1400 mailmen were let go, mostly for intemperance on the job. While mail service had slowed, Howe assured the president that within two months their replacements would be in place. There was one problem though. Twenty-three of the new applicants were women and all of them had passed the rigorous testing process.

Murmurs of disapproval were heard around the table and Howe suggested a strength test be added to avoid the unseemly result of females struggling to deliver the mail. Everyone, including Arthur, nodded in approval.

"This must be a result of that movement to get women the right to vote," opined the Secretary of State.

"Don't they have enough to worry about with childrearing and homemaking?" asked the Secretary of the Interior.

"I blame the steam-powered vacuum cleaner," said the Secretary of the Navy. "They have too much free time on their hands."

"Something needs to be done to help our Negro brothers," said Arthur, changing the subject. "First the poll taxes and now that horrific Supreme Court decision. We cannot have this kind of injustice, not under an Arthur presidency. I don't want all the good work Bob's dad did to go to waste," he said referencing Robert Todd Lincoln's father.

Arthur listed a number of proposals he wanted each of the Cabinet members to initiate to reverse this deteriorating situation, but no one was paying much attention. Without the active support of the Cabinet, it would be impossible to put pressure on Congress or the Press to initiate new legislation to aid the Negros.

The desultory Cabinet meeting was just the beginning. Arthur had lost his ability to influence the political landscape. Only a scattering of people would show up at his speeches and Congress became disinterested in the president's agenda. With the election less than two years away, there wasn't any further talk of Arthur seeking a second term. Other Republicans came to the forefront, including the scandal-prone James Blaine, whom Arthur had inherited from President Garfield as Secretary of State, but who resigned a year later to pursue his own agenda.

Arthur threw himself more and more into his trouser collection, fishing and feasting, the last of which he now usually did by himself. But after a while, Arthur sank into another depression. He started publicly berating the do-nothing members of Congress. He even threatened the Senate minority leader with a cane beating, but no one paid his excitations any attention.

During one Cabinet meeting, Arthur off-handedly suggested invading Mexico to combat the bandit incursions, but no one, not even Robert Todd Lincoln, the Secretary of War, batted an eyelash.

Afterwards Chester Alan Arthur's personal valet, Max, said that he happened to overhear what the president said about starting a war with Mexico and wondered if it was really going to happen.

"Stick to picking out my trousers," said the president gruffly.

Arthur started to abuse alcohol. Alone in his chambers one morning, he took out the pistol given to him when he was promoted to Quartermaster General during the Civil War. After putting the bullets inside the chamber, he placed the gun next to his temple and pulled the trigger. Nothing happened, however, as no one at the time had bothered to explain the role of gunpowder to the young general.

Later that afternoon, Arthur was surprised by an unannounced visit by Max. When the valet entered the room, the dog Horace growled softly. Horace never liked Max.

"How can I help you?" asked Arthur.

"Actually, I think you're the one who needs the help, Mr. President," said the valet. "Have you noticed that no one takes you legislative proposals seriously?"

"That sounds a bit impertinent, Max," said Arthur.

"I'm worried that you may try to do something. Something to overcompensate. That idea you had about invading Mexico."

"Don't worry, I was just joking," said Arthur.

"I'm concerned," said Max. "May I ask what plans you have regarding the upcoming election?"

"I haven't given it much thought to tell the truth," the president lied.

"My recommendation is not to run," said the valet. "It's time you learn what is going on, what has been happening to you over the past few months. Have you noticed the birthmark on your ankle? It's a lot darker than it used to be, isn't it?"

Arthur was speechless.

"I'm with the Monitors," said Max.

"The what?" asked Arthur.

Max went on to explain the history of the Low-Impactors and the Monitors. Max said he was assigned to monitor Arthur once it was noticed the red roots showing in the president's mutton chops.

Arthur listened in disbelief. But what the valet was saying, no matter how outrageous, at least explained what was going on.

Max explained that the Monitors had been focused on Arthur over the past few months. They had a creed never to strike down a Low-Impactor until they clearly became a threat to society. There were a few Monitors, however, who counseled a preemptive attack on Arthur. They reasoned that while many Low-Impactors tended to be people of unusual

130

talents and success, never before had a modern politician, far less a world leader, come down with the affliction. Just imagine the amount of harm such a powerful person could go unchecked. When Arthur mentioned starting a war with Mexico, some Monitors proposed assassination.

"What you mean like Garfield? Were you behind his murder as well?" asked Arthur.

"Certainly not," said the valet. "Garfield was mild mannered, but not a Low-Impactor."

A compromise was reached. As long as Arthur continued to behave in a responsible manner while in office and agreed not to seek reelection, the Monitors would let him live.

"What makes you think I want to go on living like this?" asked Arthur.

"That would be your choice," said Max, explaining that most Low-Impactors took their own lives. The valet added, however, that he personally thought it would set a disturbing precedent for the still shaky nation to have its elected leader take his own life.

"You have twenty-four hours," said Max.

Oddly, the conversation with Max buoyed Arthur's spirits. At least the valet's explanation meant Arthur wasn't losing his mind. Assassination would have sounded like a good proposition three days ago following his pathetic suicide attempt, but Arthur would rather have control over his own fortunes.

Max also had informed him of the upside to being a Low-Impactor, namely that you stopped aging. If you could avoid suicide, assassination by Monitor, or simple carelessness, you could conceivably go on living indefinitely.

So Arthur launched a plan of his own. He accepted the valet's proposition not to seek a second term, but at the same time sowed the seeds to escape the notice of the Monitors. While Low-Impactors didn't age, that didn't mean they were free of disease. Turning to his sister's copy of the *Physicians Almanac*, he settled upon a kidney ailment known as

Bright's Disease. Its symptoms included inertness and mental depression, which Arthur figured went well with his current state anyway. The disease could linger for years and then suddenly turn critical, perfect for what he had in mind.

Arthur finished out the remaining nine months of his presidential term uneventfully. Max tendered his resignation, informing the president that Low-Impactors tended to grow unusually attached to Monitors, who were the only ones who provided them with any emotional connection. Arthur informed his valet that he could not possibly grow attached to someone with even more facial hair than himself, but Max was resolute.

In the upcoming election, Arthur watched as Blaine won the Republican nomination and then lost to the Democrat Grover Cleveland. Blaine blamed his loss on Arthur, for not campaigning on his behalf, as if anyone would care about what Arthur had to say.

Perhaps out of loneliness, Arthur began to grow closer to the dog Horace, who in the past he had paid much less attention to. No one, other than Arthur, stopped to pet the dog or acknowledge its presence. Arthur wondered if it might have something to do with the dog's red hair, remembering what Max mentioned about only redheads coming down with Low-Impactor syndrome.

Instead of serving a triumphant second term, Arthur left office in obscurity, resigned to be "The Forgotten President". Upon leaving the White House, Arthur returned to his old quarters in New York, dabbled in law, and easily maintained his low profile.

One evening while walking in Greenwich Village with Horace, the dog barked sharply. Arthur heard a bullet whiz by him, as a shadowy figure disappeared into an alley. Who could possibly try to kill him? Was it a Monitor assassin from the kill-Arthur faction?

Returning home, Arthur quickly burned all his papers, including his daily journals which documented all which had gone on following that fateful meeting with his valet. He then quickly turned "ill" and provided some money to a drunkard physician, who proclaimed the ex-president dead on November 17<sup>th</sup> 1886, aged 57.

Little was mentioned in the press, although Mark Twain wrote "It would be hard indeed to better President Arthur's administration." Years later in 1935, the historian George F. Howe noted that Arthur had achieved "an obscurity in strange contrast to his significant part in American history."

He and Horace took on a new secretive lifestyle. He missed his family, particularly his daughter Nellie who was maturing into a respectable young woman, in contrast to her gallivanting older brother. Arthur would occasionally visit her, but stopped doing so, as her disinterest in seeing him broke his heart.

In the first few decades following his falsified death, Arthur appeared to have successfully given the Monitors the slip. Maintaining his muttonchops, with which he could not bear to part, he travelled the world, presenting himself as a middle-aged playboy. He had dalliances with young women, who while not interested in Arthur himself, were still quite attracted to the baubles he would bestow on them. Arthur successfully reinvented himself in the role, going by the name Chet Allen, and settling into his new life, keeping one step away from the wolf of depression.

From time to time, he would try to sort out what was causing his condition. Noticing the close resemblance of the birthmark on his ankle to a badminton shuttlecock, he learned all he could about the game, which had been invented in England around the time Arthur left office. He became proficient in the new sport, winning a number of tournaments. Arthur was never quite sure, however, whether his success at the game was due to his own talent or from a lack of competitive spirit which would afflict his competitors. One day during the summer of 1953, Arthur spotted a feature story on the sport in Life magazine. The article included the names and photos of the top U.S. badminton players. Arthur

133

was shocked to find himself included on the list, ranked sixth in the country.

A few days later while in Monaco, Arthur was enjoying a repast with a comely Italian countess. Horace growled and Arthur spotted the young women placing a dark powder into his wine glass.

"Are you trying to poison me?" Arthur asked.

"Stay away from racket sports, Mr. President," she said, before fleeing the café.

Somehow after all these years, the Monitors had once again found him. He had been out of office nearly three-quarters of a century. Couldn't they just let him live his obscure life in peace?

Boarding the next plane back to New York, he thought of an even more secretive lifestyle which would suit him. In recent years a new kind of habitation had gained favor, where elderly people could stay without being a burden to their families. These institutions came with all of Arthur's favorite amenities, including the newly popular contraption known as television.

Arthur always liked the Florida climate, and so he enrolled himself into Sunny Bright Retirement Village in Clearwater. There he managed to fade once again from the Monitors and maintain a lifestyle to his liking. Horace the dog accompanied him there, but would take off on his own on occasion, sometimes for months at time.

One day Horace returned to Sunny Bright not alone, but with two young redheads, a man who looked somewhat familiar and a woman who looked like Pippi Longstocking, but with dental headgear. Claiming they were afflicted by the same condition as Arthur, the duo suggested that he leave Sunny Bright with them. For the first time in over a century, except for when he was with Horace, Arthur no longer felt alone. Still, he was not about to leave his safety zone of Sunny Bright Manor to throw in with this intriguing duo, especially after the woman mentioned that they were on the run from the Monitors. But when she said that another member of their squad was able to track him down via the Internet, Arthur realized there was nothing to stop the Monitors from doing the same. Anyone with enough computer skills could locate him and would realize that it was not quite normal for someone to remain at the same assisted living facility for 64 years.

Something definitely was changing. Low-Impactors were beginning to recognize other Low-Impactors. Even more peculiar, Arthur's birthmark, which had remained pitch black for the past 90 years, had started fluctuating in color again. And in the rare instances when it would grow whitish, the other residents of Sunny Bright would listen to what he had to say. Overcoming his caution, Arthur decided to throw in with the young redheads. Perhaps his political career was not yet over after all.

# CHAPTER THIRTEEN

The puppy was scared. He was being picked up roughly by a boy. He tried to wiggle free, but the boy was too strong.

"I like this one with the white mark on his tummy," said the boy in common Gaelic.

The puppy cried for three full nights, but over time he grew to love his new human family, especially the boy with whom he chased, played, and did tug-of-war. The boy was sometimes mean, like when he placed a sheet over the puppy so the puppy couldn't see what he was doing, or when he'd pull on the puppy's tail. But the puppy was also sometimes mean, like when he would steal the boy's favorite toys and run around the house with them.

As the puppy grew into a dog, his job was to mind the sheep around the farm and keep them together where they belonged. "Not bad for a Setter," said the boy's father. The year was 1576 and there were still wolf packs prowling the countryside. Occasionally, one would try to attack a stray sheep near the woods edge, but the dog was too fast and strong for a lone wolf.

The dog's favorite thing, other than tug-of-war, was the monthly bird hunt. "Easy, easy boy!" said the man, as the dog ran around faster and faster his tail knocking over anything in the way, including the smallest member of the family, an 11-month old girl just learning how to walk. Once outside, the dog could smell and hear a bird before the man and the boy. He'd point out where the bird was located and bound out to retrieve it.

He was not the only dog in the Irish village, and was interested in the markings left by females, informing him of their availability. There were also markings of males, sometimes outrageously deposited right on top of his own. The dog felt good and knew his place both with his human family and with other canines in the village.

One day the dog was outside playing with the small girl, the one he had a habit of knocking over. It was winter and food was tough to come by. From around the woods surrounding the house, the dog smelled and then saw the wolf-pack, ears down.

The pack leader charged straight for the girl. The dog tried to protect her, but the wolf already had the girl's leg. The dog pulled the wolf off, biting into its unprotected underside. Others in the pack joined in, some attacking the dog, but others the girl. Luckily, the father emerged with a new hunting weapon, the one which made a lot of noise. Sensing the battle odds shift, the pack quickly dispersed.

"He saved Aine's life," the father told the family. "He's a very brave dog."

That night the dog received a lot of belly-rubs and got to eat the same meat as the rest of the family. And he got to play tug-of-war with the man. The man pulled much harder than the boy, lifting the dog into the air around and around. But the dog did not let go and ruin his lifetime unbeaten streak at tug-of-war.

One day the dog woke up feeling tired and groggy. "His nose is dry and hot!" announced the boy to the family, when he noticed the dog was not eating that morning. The boy tried to cheer him up by bringing his favorite rope toy, but the dog could only muster a few half-hearted tugs. The boy also tried giving a belly-rub. "His mark is really dark," said the boy, referencing the odd-shaped birthmark visible through the sparse fur on the dog's stomach. The dog dragged himself outside to tend to the sheep, but for the first time in his four years, he didn't feel up to the task, even letting a couple of the sheep stray near the woods line.

Dragging himself back into the house at the end of the day, the dog was surprised to find his food was not out yet, not that he had much appetite anyway. Furthermore, his water was the same as in the morning, not fresh. The dog suddenly felt an urge, an urge he knew had to wait until going outside. But the door was closed. He nudged the woman like he normally did to signal his need, but she was preoccupied with feeding the small girl he had rescued. The dog didn't want to make a mistake within the house, no matter how badly he was feeling. That was what puppies did.

Finally, he could control himself no longer. Shamed, he hid in the closet, waiting the discovery. The accident was indeed discovered by the woman, who set to work cleaning it up. However, she did not yell at the dog. Nor did any of the other family members. Maybe this was a new form of punishment, so heinous was his crime? Maybe they were going to kick him out of the family? Whimpering, the dog, slunk over to his bed and closed his eyes.

The next morning he was feeling better. However, the marking on his belly was darker and it itched. He tried licking it, but to no avail. He then saw the boy and the man getting on their hunting clothes. It was birding day! He ran around wildly, barking. But no one tried to calm him down.

Smelling a pheasant 200 yards to the northeast, the dog pointed to the hidden prey. But the humans and continued in the wrong direction. Once by pure luck, the man was able to shoot a thrush who they happened to stumble upon. The bird was wounded and flew off a few hundred yards before crashing into the underbrush. The dog raced to the scene, quickly dispatching the bird and bringing it back to the hunting party. But no one cared. The dog dropped the dead bird in the field and spent the rest of the day tagging behind the rest of the party.

Returning home, the dog found no food or water in his bowls. He went outside and drank from the dirty puddle outside the back door and scrounged leftovers from the garbage. The scent markings left by the other dogs no longer included him. No female marked her interest and his overmarks were left untouched by the other males.

Back at the house, the dog licked the boy's face. But the boy did not laugh or push the dog off and try to get his tail. This time, the boy nudged the dog aside and went back to playing alone with his toy soldiers.

Fortunately, the dog did not go hungry. He would jump up onto the kitchen table and take whatever food he wanted without punishment. He also found out he could hunt rabbits and other small game outside. They didn't care enough to run away.

During one of his outings into the woods, the dog stumbled right into the wolf den, which was located downwind. The troop numbered nine adults as well as four pups. This was a deadly situation—wolves were highly intelligent, nearly as smart as the dog and certainly much smarter than any of the other village dogs.

The dog attacked the pack leader, biting him repeatedly, but received not even a growl in response. He bit one of the pups, which gave out a sharp squeak. The mother wolf licked the pup but ignored the dog. Confused by their inaction, he went to the throat of the pack leader. It whined slightly, but still remained passive. The dog considered finishing off the wolf, but instead let it live.

The dog sensed a change in his body, or rather a lack of change. The small degradations which normally occur as the body ages, no longer were occurring within the dog. He could still get injured, however, as when a sharp rock cut his left front paw, causing him to hop on his remaining three legs for two days. In order to avoid further such unpleasantries, the dog took to a rather inactive life, one more appropriate for a sick or very old dog.

What is supposed to happen that the family dog grows old and eventually dies, leaving the family heartbroken. With this particular dog, however, it was the reverse. Over the years, the members of the family grew older, not the dog. Other members of the family disappeared one by one, either from illness, injury or disease. Some also moved away, but some including the boy, who by now had become a man, remained.

New family members were born, but the dog did not have the same bond to them as to the original family, whom he still remembered from when they once praised, played, fed and groomed him. He hoped someday they might remember him once again and every now and then, when his shuttlecock shaped marking temporarily grew a bit lighter in color, the boy would absently pat the dog.

When the old man, who was once the boy, passed away, the dog decided to set off to find a new home which didn't make him so sad. His travels took him throughout Ireland.

Every once in a while he would encounter someone, either canine or human, who smelled different. The dog would seek these individuals out, as they would notice him! But the canines would growl and snap at him and the humans would shoo him away or throw bottles or rocks at him. The dog eventually learned to give a wide berth to individuals who smelled like this. These individuals were what humans with his condition would call "Monitors."

At times, he would smell others who he instinctively could tell were "like me". He remembered his first encounter with a fellow Low-Impactor in Dublin in 1784. The man was wandering the streets intoxicated on rye whisky. The dog barked, wagging his tail, and ran in tighter and tighter circles around the man. But the man paid him no attention. The dog continued to trail the man, but the next day, the man jumped to his death off of a bridge overlooking the Liffy.

Most of these unusual humans didn't live very long, succumbing to accidents, or more usually suicide. A very few, however, thought there may be a place, somewhere in the world where they might yet matter once again. One such individual stowed away on a boat which had set sail to New York and the dog hopped on along with him.

Sometimes a Low-Impactor would try to hurt other human beings, but these rare Low-Impactors were quickly killed by a Monitor. Perhaps due to his new condition, the dog's sense of smell towards both Low-Impactors and Monitors became unusually acute, spanning hundreds of miles.

Occasionally the dog would also encounter Low-Impactor Irish Setters such as himself. He would try to make their acquaintance, but found them no better at noticing him than regular dogs. Their life expectancies were also very short, either falling prey to accidents or failing to eat enough to sustain themselves.

One day in the fall of 1882, while roaming the streets of Baltimore, a strong but distant scent wafted into the dog's nostrils. It was another Low-Impactor, but somehow different. This individual had not yet had the full impact of the condition manifest itself. The dog headed off to the direction of this new, interesting smell, hopping on a freight train going in that direction. Along with his heightened sense of smell for both Low-Impactors and Monitors, the dog's tracking ability increased commensurately, and he was able to determine the fastest and safest route to his destination. The city he was heading towards was named Washington, D.C.

He found his way into a huge room within a building with a domed roof filled entirely with male humans. This room was the chamber of the House of Representatives within the U.S. Congress. The occasion was the annual State of the Union address and the man giving off the scent was speaking. His name was Chester Alan Arthur and he was the President of the United States.

Now normally a dog wouldn't be able to walk into a State of the Union address, even in the 19th century, but of course, the dog didn't receive the attention of a normal dog. The address focused on the Pendleton Civil Service Reform Act, which the president was supporting, to the consternation of his closest political allies. Perhaps due to the unusually light color of the president's shuttlecock birthmark, the chamber erupted in applause from both sides of the aisle. It was the best speech of President Arthur's political career and instrumental in passing the legislation which outlawed nepotism within the federal government.

The dog took up residence within the White House. Chester Alan Arthur at first didn't notice him any more than anyone else, but one day, when the dog's own shuttlecock marking was unusually light, the President asked, "Who let this dog in here?"

"I will escort it out," said the White House butler.

"No, that won't be necessary. I might like a dog," The president added, "I'm going to name him Horace."

Horace jumped up onto the president and began licking his face, tasting the crumbs of the president's most recent repast stuck in his massive muttonchops.

"This dog is badly in need of a bath," said the president.

Years later, Horace sensed something new. The scent of Chester Alan Arthur as well as that for some other Low-Impactors had changed. For the first time in centuries, an instinct in Horace returned—the desire to herd. For everyone's protection, the Low-Impactors needed to get together and it was up to Horace to help them do so.

# CHAPTER FOURTEEN

After packing up Arthur's things, mostly trousers, they all piled into the yellow convertible, Angela at the wheel with Tad riding shotgun and Arthur and Horace crammed into the back.

As they merged onto the interstate, Maurice's face came up on Angela's cellphone. "Any luck Professor?" he asked.

"Yes, Chet has agreed to come back with us," said Angela. "And you won't believe—"

"Professor?" Tad asked.

"That's an exaggeration," said Angela. "I'm actually just a graduate student … of astrophysics … at Princeton."

"Angela is a genius," said Maurice. "Didn't you know that?"

"I thought you were a failed waitress," Tad said to Angela.

"That's also true. I needed money for my student loans."

"So, you mean to say you're actually smart?" asked Tad.

"At some things," Angela replied.

"Smart girls tend to like me," said Tad.

"You're way too old for me," Angela replied.

"I'm two years younger than you are."

"Precisely."

"Did you know that Angela is a genius?" Tad asked. Glancing to the back seat. Tad spotted Chester Alan Arthur and Horace apparently asleep, the latter with his head resting in the ex-president's lap

"Not surprising," said Arthur, through closed eyes.

"I'll be awaiting your arrival," said Maurice, ending the call.

Having a few hours to kill before the next flight back to San Jose, Angela suggested they make a quick detour to the beach.

"I didn't pack a bathing suit," said Tad, as Angela accelerated onto the lane marked "Beaches."

Tad did not like beaches, in part because his fair skin burned so easily. He always missed sunscreen on major sections of his body and had to go around sporting red splotches for a week afterwards.

"Who's going to notice?" asked Angela.

Pulling the car onto the sand, Angela hopped out of the car and removed her rhinestone "Angela!" t-shirt and denim cutoffs, leaving on only her bra and panties. Tad also exited the vehicle, with Chester Alan Arthur and Horace tumbling out the back.

As Tad stripped down to his boxers and t-shirt, Angela remarked, "You were really cut in *Hopalong Cannibal*."

"Thanks," said Tad as Angela ran into the water, letting slide the implied slight to his current physique.

Arthur removed his Armani straight-leg jersey trousers revealing a white Speedo.

At 6' 3" and built like a linebacker, Arthur towered half a head above Tad, not exactly the broken down old man he appeared to be at Sunny Bright.

Meanwhile, Angela was already returning from her dip. With the sun behind her, she reminded Tad of Halle Berry in that James Bond beach scene, except of course for the glare coming off her orthodontic headgear.

"You like her," said Arthur.

"No," said Tad.

"Great bathing suit," Angela said to Arthur. "Could you put some sunscreen on me?"

"Certainly," said Arthur.

"Do you need some?" Arthur asked Tad.

"I'll do it myself," Tad replied.

Horace began barking at an unclaimed beach volleyball. He tried to get his mouth around it, but the ball was too big.

"Let's play!" Angela said, scooping up the ball and heading towards a vacant court with the others following close behind.

Angela and Tad went to the far side with Arthur facing off across the net. Angela served the ball and Arthur returned it with surprising agility. Horace, meanwhile, played both sides of the court, awaiting a mistake. After a few more hits back and forth, Arthur scored with a thunderous spike, barely missing Tad's head.

In the process, however, Arthur tripped over Horace and fell headlong into the sand.

"President Arthur!" Angela exclaimed.

A few beach bunnies from a neighboring court gathered around him.

"Are you alright?" asked a blonde. A brunette began applying mouth-to-mouth resuscitation.

As the ex-president struggled back to his feet, a cheer went up among the women. Horace began barking excitedly. The shuttlecock on Chester Alan Arthur's left ankle was blazing bright white.

# SNEAK PEAK (FROM BOOK TWO OF THE SHUTTLECOCKS SERIES)

Cheers went up among the people piled into Times Square.

"They're asking for you!" said Ryan Seacrest sitting in the broadcast booth, grinning at the large man sitting next to him wearing Valentino side stripe twill chinos. The man fluffed his muttonchops, causing a new wave of cheers.

"We need to take a quick break, but we'll be right back with *New Year's Rockin' Eve* with Chet Allen and me, Ryan Seacrest!"

Seacrest's Cheshire cat smile faded. "You forgot my close-up," he informed the camera man.

#

"We're down to two minutes," exclaimed Seacrest, following the commercial break. "Are you excited?"

"Yes, I am," replied Chester Alan Arthur.

"You know I have to ask it," said Seacrest, glancing sidelong at Arthur.

"What's that?" asked Arthur, causing a wave of laughter from the crowd.

"You know what I'm talking about," smiled Seacrest, poking Arthur's arm. "Are you going to run?"

Arthur raised an eyebrow, eliciting more laughter.

"Who wants Chet Allen to run for president?" asked Seacrest. A roar went up from the crowd.

#

"Initiate Shuttlecock Annihilation Protocol," said the Chairman of the Monitors, turning off the TV.

# ABOUT THE AUTHOR

Brian Harris is a writer of both humorous non-fiction and plays. He co-wrote *Lay Low and Don't Make the Big Mistake*, a business humor book published by Simon and Schuster, as well as the Off-Broadway dark comedy *Tall Grass*, published by Samuel French. His plays have won awards in NY theater, including winning the *Strawberry One-Act Festival* twice and the Jean Dalrymple Award for Best Comedy Playwright. He has an MBA for the University of Chicago and worked most of his career as a Wall Street analyst covering the airline sector. He lives in Miami Beach with his wife, daughter and puppy. He is currently at work on the sequel to *Calling Mr. Beige*. He can be contacted at brian@harriswordforge.com or find him on Facebook at Harris Word Forge.

Made in the USA
Lexington, KY
21 June 2017